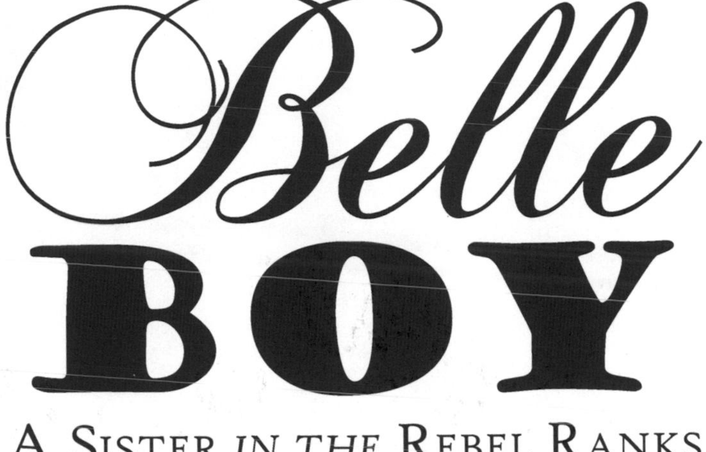

A Sister *in the* Rebel Ranks

A NOVEL

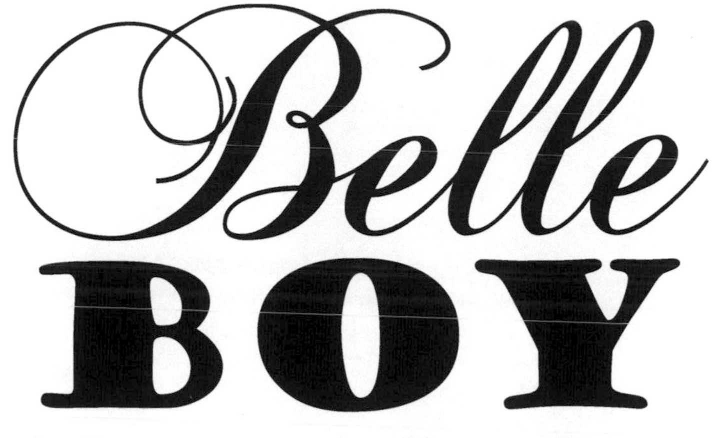

A Sister *in the* Rebel Ranks

A Novel

Anne Fuller

Omaha, Nebraska

ISBN10: 0-9827430-1-7
ISBN13: 978-0-9827430-1-0
Library of Congress Control Number: 2010930413
Cataloging in Publication Data on file with publisher.

Fuller Minds, LLC
P.O. Box 391415
Omaha, Nebraska 68139
www.FullerMinds.com

Book Design: Gary James Withrow
Production and Marketing: Concierge Marketing, Inc.
www.ConciergeMarketing.com

Printed in the United States of America
10 9 8 7 6 5 4 3 2 1

To the two men who never doubted,
my dad and my husband

ACKNOWLEDGMENTS

Creating a book is a long and interesting group project. While my name is on the cover, this book would not exist without the help of several people. I never would have had the idea for the plot, or attempted the book without reading *They Fought like Demons* by Deanne Blanton and Lauren M. Cook and *Red Clay to Richmond* by John J. Fox, III.

The team at Concierge Marketing has been invaluable with their knowledge and talents in taking a manuscript and a dream and making it a published book on the market. Thanks go to Lisa Pelto, book publishing guru, who had the knowledge to lead me through this project. Thank you to Gary Withrow for the most beautiful cover I've ever seen and all his patience through the design stages. I also appreciate all the help given me by Erin Pankowski, and Ellie Pelto for figuring out paperwork, marketing, appointments and many other necessary items—in addition to encouraging me all along the way that this was a story people would love. Special thanks to Monica Pelto for finding the title when no one else could see it. My editor, Joyce Whitfield, made this a much better book and was very patient in leading me through the revising process. Thank you to Emmalee Briggs, Gaylin Fuller, Jackie Polacek, Kylie Wideseth, and Sandra Wendel, for your input after reading the manuscript. Laroe Adams at Fort Jackson, Savannah, Georgia, answered my many questions about Civil War infantry life and commands. I appreciate his willingness to spend the afternoon talking with me. Thanks to Jason Harper, D.O. for talking with me about hip wounds during the Civil War. Even with all these wonderful sources, mistakes will be found—those mistakes are mine alone. Let us know if there is an error and we'll fix it next time we print.

Thank you especially to my intelligent and amazing children—Lisa, for reading every single revision (well, except for one); and to Rob, Emma, and Cody for experiencing every up and down with me and being dragged to more Civil War battlegrounds, visitor's centers, and camp sites than they probably ever wanted to see. Most especially thank you to Mark, for always being there and helping me see this story through. Without him there would not have been a book at all. Finally, I have received the support and encouragement from countless family members and friends. You know who you are, and I thank you.

AUTHOR'S NOTE

The Civil War took place from 1861-1865. At this point in American history, women were not allowed to vote, they did not go to college, and they absolutely did not fight in wars—or so everyone thought. Evidence shows there were women who traded in their skirts for uniforms; but for many years both sides of the conflict denied any known female soldiers.

There were, in fact, several women who went to battle in the Civil War. Actual numbers are not known, because the women who left home to join the fight assumed men's names, and many were never discovered. It is currently believed there were around 400 women serving under assumed names between the Union and the Confederate armies. Experts and historians believe that records will never reflect an exact count.

Why did the men not notice? A common theory is that women were not expected to be seen in uniform (remember that at this time all women wore dresses), so the men in camp saw what they expected to see—another man. Another theory is that the idea of women fighting was so foreign the men couldn't recognize a female soldier.

One of my favorite true stories of a woman in the Civil War is that of Jennie Hodgers, a.k.a. Albert Cashier. She joined the union army in 1862 and was assigned to the 90th Illinois. In the summer of 1865 her regiment was disbanded and in her hometown "Albert" received a standing ovation for fighting. It should be noted that no one in her hometown knew she was a woman since she began her masquerade before she had moved there. She continued to masquerade as a man for the next 42 years and even received an invalid soldier's pension before she was discovered. If you would like to read more about "Albert," read the book They Fought Like Demons by Deanne Blanton and Lauren M. Cook.

There are also several instances of women joining up with husbands, brothers, or fathers to go to war. After their relative was killed in battle, they admitted to their commanding officer their true gender—there was no reason to stay once their loved one was gone.

Modern excavations of the mass graves from the Civil War have revealed skeletons that scientists believe are women as evidenced by their smaller bone structure and other gender-identifying differences. This evidence underlines the fact that we will never truly know how many women disguised themselves and fought during the Civil War.

I spend many of my days researching and reading about the Civil War; and I often dream and wonder about these women who joined the armed forces during this difficult war. They went against the expectations of the time and lived through much hardship. How would it have been and would it have been worth it to change your whole identity to fight in the Civil War?

Thank you for joining me for this story. I hope you enjoy reading about Samantha Anne as much as I enjoyed writing about her! Feel free to write to me if you have any questions about the characters in this book.

PROLOGUE

Gwinnett County, Georgia
July 1863

The sound of hooves could be heard on the hard packed dirt of the drive in front of the house. I went to the top of the stairs to see my father coming through the big front door. I gathered the skirt of my worn nightgown and ran down the steps to him.

Meeting him on the threshold I grabbed his arm and asked impatiently, "What did you find out? Where is he?"

For a moment Father's gray eyes looked blankly into mine and I could see the worried lines etched in his gaunt face. His face had once been full and vital; it was now tired and bleak.

"Samantha Anne," Mother's voice—full of disapproval—came from the doorway of the parlor behind me. "A lady does not clutch at a gentleman, nor does she come downstairs in her night clothes!"

I turned to look at my mother with her grim face, her lips pulled into a tight line of irritation, her hair pulled severely back from her face, her dress impeccable despite the lateness of the hour. My mother often scolded and corrected me. Usually, I would have been upset at my mother's words, but tonight I knew her sharpness was rooted in the same anxiety I was feeling. We were both anxious over the unknown whereabouts of my older brother.

My three older sisters were everything my mother wanted in daughters. Girls who loved to play with their dolls and have tea parties with miniature china tea sets. As they got older, they took Mother's lessons on what was proper very seriously. All had grown into genteel young ladies who had further pleased Mother by entering excellent marriages with highly eligible men.

When the youngest of my sisters was seven, my brother, Johnny, was born. Since my parents had given up hope of having any more children, he was doted on shamelessly by the entire family. Part of this devotion was due to the fact that he was the son both my father and mother had always wanted. Imagine everyone's surprise when three years later I was born.

Since Johnny and I were so close in age, it was natural for me to shadow and imitate Johnny rather than my older sisters. Besides, they were much more interested in hairstyles and the fashion of their dresses than whatever their baby sister might want to play. As a result, I'd spend my time fishing, climbing trees, and preferring mud pies over pretend teacakes.

Johnny and I were great friends, and that friendship didn't change even as we got older and our interests diverged. Mine, even shocking myself, to hairstyles and his to the rumors of a possible armed battle with the North.

When the South started mustering regiments to fight in the battle for state's rights, Johnny joined up as soon as he could. Thinking it would be a short time before I'd see him again, I laughingly told him to get a Yank for me. In my naiveté about battle, I didn't really realize what I was telling him. Johnny had lamented he was so late already that he'd probably never see any action at all.

Months turned into years. What I thought would be a few small battles became a war, full of worry for those of us still at home. Johnny continued to write letters, and he had even come home for furlough a couple of times. Furloughs were leaves of absence granted by the army to the soldiers. Every soldier's family looked forward to his furlough, especially since they were granted infrequently.

When Johnny came home, I found that my handsome, reckless, and somewhat spoiled brother was growing up. He was still handsome and fun, but there was a new seriousness in his eyes and in the letters he sent home. After every rumored battle, we waited impatiently for news—casualty lists or a letter from a commander or comrade that something had happened.

Johnny wrote often and usually soon after a battle. We knew by the receipt of his letter that he had come through another conflict unharmed. However, after the news of a horrible battle in Gettysburg, Pennsylvania, we didn't get the usual reassuring letter from my brother. Instead, in the newspaper under the heading "Missing in Action" was my brother's name: Jonathon Davis, Georgia 35th Infantry.

I was horrified and devastated. Seeing Johnny's name listed in that newspaper meant no one knew where my brother was. He could be in some prison behind Yankee lines, he could be in a hospital—unconscious and injured with other hurt men. Or he could be in a mass grave of unknown Confederate soldiers buried somewhere in Pennsylvania.

I didn't let myself dwell on the last option because I believed in my heart Johnny was alive. My father believed it too, and had just spent several days tracking every lead he could find. I had hoped that when he came home tonight, he would be able to tell us where he'd found Johnny.

"I didn't find him," Father answered, ignoring what Mother and I had just said. "I went to everyone I could, pulled all the favors I was owed and still I have no idea where Johnny might be."

Mother came over and took Father's arm, the one that I was not already holding. She gently said, "Come, Jacob, come and sit. We'll get you something warm to drink and you can tell us all about it."

Together we steered him into the parlor and helped him sit down on the worn couch. Mother sat next to him and patted the stiff fingers of his right hand. "Now, tell us what you found out about Johnny."

Father shook his head. "No one knows where Johnny is. I went as far up the chain of command as I could. Did you know there is even a department in the army whose only job is to locate the lost and the wounded? They are trying to locate so many lost men, they haven't even started thinking about the lists that have come out from Gettysburg."

Father continued bitterly. "I've asked a hundred questions, but everything is in an uproar. There are more wounded than the doctors can handle. With supply problems and not enough men to fulfill the army's needs, very few people—even those who are friends—have time to address the demands of so many families. Johnny is just one of many who is missing in action.

"Some have deserted no doubt, and some are wounded. The records are a mess, but most of the missing are either dead on a battlefield somewhere or in a prison camp up North. No one wants to say it, but it is as clear as day that everyone I talked to thinks that we won't ever see Johnny again."

I was reeling with shock and discouragement. I had been sure Father would find out something—anything.

Father went on, massaging his stiff right hand. "If it weren't for this bum hand of mine, I'd join up and find him myself."

"How, Father?" I asked.

Mother interrupted, "Samantha Anne, go to the kitchen and ask Hettie to make up a pot of coffee for your father! Tell her she can use the last of the coffee that we have been saving. We might as well drink it up."

Hettie was one of our servants. She'd been with the family since before I was born. Every time my parents wanted me out of the way, they sent me to run an errand. I wanted to hear whatever Father and Mother were going to say next.

"Yes, Mother," I replied meekly and headed out the parlor door.

Upon leaving the parlor, I dragged my feet. I waited to see if Father's comment would be explained. I didn't have to wait long before I heard Mother say, "Jacob, you could not have found out any more by joining up."

"Yes I could have!" replied my father. "I would have gotten as close to his regiment as possible. Others were out there with Johnny during the fighting. They would have seen him. If we could find out what happened there on the field, there is a chance we could determine where he went from there. A twenty-two-year-old man does not just disappear."

"I thought you had a letter sent to Frank asking if he had seen Johnny during the battle."

"My brother hasn't seen fit to reply."

Deep in thought, I walked back to the kitchen and found Hettie. I told her Mother wanted coffee for Father. This would be our last pot of coffee, and it would be weak and taste odd since we hadn't been drinking real coffee for months due to the war. No one could get coffee anymore. As Hettie began making the coffee, I went up the back stairs to my room. I was thinking about what Father had said.

The army wouldn't take Father because his right hand was completely immobile from a hunting accident that had occurred when he was a boy. His left hand was incredibly stiff due to painfully swollen joints. He did as much as he could with his left hand, but it was difficult for him to grasp anything. There was little chance that he would be able to pull the trigger on a musket.

The army was taking almost anyone they could get—young boys and old men. From what I could tell by the men who were being drafted from the area, you just had to be able to load and fire a gun to get in.

When I reached my room, I looked in the mirror and pulled my hair up behind my head. I had braided my straight, long hair before I went to bed last night, and now I studied myself critically. My eyes were gray like Father's. I had just a dusting of freckles over the tip of my nose, which had concerned me before the war started. But then I had come to know there were things that were really important to worry about, and freckles wasn't one of them. Not when loved ones were fighting and dying and food was scarce.

My hair was thick, a deep dark brown without any wave or curl. I would not have described myself as beautiful or even overly feminine looking. Taking a more critical look at myself, I felt a bolt of confidence that I could pass for an adventurous boy. True, I wasn't as tall as most boys my age, but I could probably pass for a fourteen-year-old boy. Father couldn't go into the army, but I could.

ꕤ

I started my transformation from nineteen-year-old girl to fourteen-year-old boy by digging through Johnny's chest of drawers. I found an old pair of pants and a shirt that fit me decently. They were a little big, but I figured big was better than too tight. With baggy clothes, no one would be able to tell that I had curves in all the wrong places. Just to be sure, I wound a long piece of soft cloth around my chest, binding myself to look more like a man.

Next, I took a pair of sharp scissors and, with a small sigh of regret, chopped off the two braids on each side of my head. My thick brown hair was my one true vanity, even if it wouldn't hold a curl for any length of time. The cropped locks on my head were uneven and choppy, making me look like a scarecrow—but it would be worth it if I could locate my big brother.

As I trimmed at the remnants of my hair, working for a smoother style, I pondered on what name I should give to the army. As desperate as the army was for soldiers, they were not accepting girls.

Christopher? Snip. *No, I'll never remember to answer to that.* Snip, snip. *Think of one closer to Samantha.* Snip. *Steven?* Snip. *I'm not sure I'd remember to answer to that.* Snip, snip. *Stanley?* Snip. *At least that is closer to Sam...* Pause, the scissors hovering at my hairline. *Naturally, Sam. Johnny always called me Sammie Annie; now I'll be Samuel.*

Pleased with my decision I finished working on my hair. The effort was not entirely successful, but I felt I looked more boy than girl now.

Finally, after pulling on the smallest pair of boots I could find in Johnny's closet, and packing a few necessary things in an old knapsack, I shoved a cap over my now short hair and tiptoed to the kitchen.

The kitchen was dark, so Hettie must have gone to bed. I scrounged up some food from the pantry, left a note to Mother and Father in the middle of the table, and snuck out the back door into the night. I was on my way to join the Confederate army in hopes of finding my older brother, Johnny Davis.

ONE

~

Orange County Court House
August 1863

The knots in my belly tightened at the sound of the drums coming closer. I was glad that I was in the third row toward the back of the formation. I wouldn't be able to see much because the man I lined up behind was taller than me. As ordered, we had formed into a hollow, three-sided square. The fourth side of the square was where the executions were to take place. The men from my regiment had seemed particularly subdued all morning. I had learned that one of the men to be executed had belonged to the Georgia 14th Infantry, my new regiment. While the sentence of this man's court-martial had been handed down right before I'd arrived at the camp around Orange County Court House, I could feel and relate to the grief and the anger some of my comrades were experiencing.

I had been with my new regiment for less than a week. I now was experiencing some very serious doubts about my plan to find Johnny by dressing up as a soldier and looking for him with his old battalion. I'd gotten as close as I could to his regiment without actually joining it.

Johnny had been a member of the Georgia 35th Infantry, which I couldn't outright join because several of my relatives were in the 35th. I wasn't convinced they would keep my gender a secret. I also reasoned that it would be dangerous to join Johnny's same regiment because I wasn't sure how many of his peers knew about his family. They could have remembered that Johnny didn't have any younger brothers, just a younger sister.

The men of the Georgia 14th knew Johnny but not well enough that they would have known details of his family that might call for an explanation of a younger brother instead of a younger sister. The two regiments had also been fighting—or campaigning—together forever, as far as I could tell from the newspapers and Johnny's letters.

Actually, enlisting had proven much easier than I had thought it would be. The recruiting officer gave me a bit of a scare. I'd gone in and stated that I was ready to join up.

He'd looked me up and down with a skeptical eye and asked, "How old are you, boy? There isn't any way you'll convince me that you're past seventeen." I was already nineteen, but I didn't think I could convince him that a nineteen-year-old boy didn't have a smidgen of facial hair.

I simply answered with complete truth, "I've already had my seventeenth birthday, sir."

He looked me over again, making me very uncomfortable, and glanced at the mountain of papers on his desk. Then he gave me a broad wink and said, "Sure you're seventeen, boy."

I stood in breathless silence for a minute while he waited for me to retract my statement. When I didn't say anything, he shrugged his shoulders and said, "We need everyone we can get. If the surgeon says you're fit to fight, you can go find your adventure, boy."

He sent me on to the surgeon, and I was convinced the surgeon would expose me and put a stop to the whole thing. The surgeon did not say anything, just looked me up and down, told me to open my mouth so he could see my teeth, and then he signed the papers to "send me on."

"Send me on" meant being sent to basic training at Fort Randolph where my real uncertainty with the scheme to find Johnny would really begin.

ଓ

The training was rigorous for the men who were there, but I was learning more than how to recognize the commands from the bugler and the series of drills and formations.

I was learning how to act like a man. I realized quickly that it would take more than short hair and Johnny's cast-off clothing to convince people that I was a young man with an adventurous spirit who joined the Confederate army.

I learned the deception had to be more than skin deep the first night at Fort Randolph when another young man about my age started making fun of the way I walked.

"Look at that girly walk!" he hooted, laughing with a couple of other recruits who were with him.

I'd spent enough time in the company of boys to know I had to respond, so I just sneered and said, "I'd rather walk like a girl than look like one."

Recognizing the insult for what it was—a direct challenge and one that I was none too sure I wanted to issue—my insulter said, "You talkin' to me, boy?"

"You look in the mirror lately? Maybe if you did, you'd know whether I was talking to you or not!" I responded with false confidence.

The young man had fisted his hands and was advancing menacingly when the call for dinner was made. One of his friends had pushed him toward the mess (where all the meals were served) and said, "C'mon Clint, this puny kid ain't worth it."

To my relief, Clint backed off, sneered at me, and said, "Naw, he ain't." The group had all headed toward the mess, but I stayed, studying the way they walked. Sure enough. There was a distinct difference in their stride and in the stride of ladies, which I'd never really noticed before.

Boys didn't sway when they walked. They strode forward from the hip, keeping their legs directly under their hips and using only their legs to eat up the distance over the ground. Their hips and upper body hardly moved at all as a result of their taking a step.

I also decided as I studied Clint walk away that they didn't swing their lower leg as much from the knee as girls tended to. Starting right then, I worked on walking more like the boys did. By the time I left Fort Randolph three weeks later, walking like a boy was such a habit I didn't even have to think to do it right.

I also realized while at Fort Randolph I always had to act like a man—always. One week after I'd arrived at the Fort, a couple of females were discovered pretending to be soldiers. The way they were discovered was foolish, and it made me quiver with nervousness to realize just how easily I could be unmasked myself.

A recruit tossed an apple to one of the two females who were standing near one another. He threw it straight at her face, and she turned her back with a little shriek that was several octaves too high. Obviously, she had never tried to catch anything before.

The other female was detailed with me and a few others to unload a wagon of supplies that had come in. She and another soldier were to climb into the wagon and pass the supplies out to those of us on the ground. After the first soldier got into the wagon, she reached her right arm up to be helped in the wagon. As she stretched for help, her left hand reached to control her skirt for climbing into the wagon bed. All of this happened in one fluid motion. The sequence of her actions were so clear to everyone who had witnessed it that no one could doubt she was not a he.

Both females were sent to the commanding officer. They were lucky in that he just sent them home. At that time, I learned of other women who had been discovered and had been sent to prison.

☙

By the time I arrived at Orange County Court House to join the 14th, I was sure my time in the army would be short as I was bound to be found out. Surprisingly, once at the camp I was completely accepted as a boy, which should have made me ecstatic that my plan was working.

Instead, I was miserable and in daily dread of being discovered. I had finally realized that for all my tomboyish ways, I really liked being a lady and all the privileges that went along with being a lady—even in difficult times.

My sergeant didn't like me in the least, and while on parade—a daily ritual where we marched in formation and were inspected by our superior officers—and doing drills, he was constantly barking at me. To be fair, he barked at everyone a lot and at those of us new to the camp the most.

The sergeant wasn't the worst, though; that was Mac, a man in my regiment. He had been in the 14th from the first call to arms and he didn't even try to hide his contempt for "greenies" or "Johnny Raws" much, mostly because of our inexperience.

Mac wasn't the only one who didn't like those of us who had just arrived at the front, but he was by far the most obvious in his contempt for me. He needled me whenever he could, painting horrible pictures of battle and saying that a baby like me wouldn't last a minute. The company didn't have time to babysit; why didn't I go back home to my mama?

If there was a chance to trip me or knock me down, Mac would take it. I avoided him as much as I possibly could, but the more I tried to avoid Mac, the more he tried to seek me out. For some reason, he seemed to like to pick on me even more than on the other recruits who had arrived at the same time I did. Another veteran—the name given to the men who had been in the army long enough to see a real battle—named Tom, took me under his wing. He had known Johnny and heard that I was trying to piece together what had happened to him. Tom put up with my questions, but he shook his head at my foolishness.

I hadn't made any headway on locating Johnny in the five weeks since I'd left home. I was sore and hungry (even if I did have more meat on my bones than all the men who had been in camp longer than two weeks). Besides living in constant fear of being unmasked, the camp was disgusting and I was discouraged.

ଓ

This execution was the final straw for me. *What was I doing here? Who did I think I was that I could fool the entire Confederate army, find my brother when no one else was able to, and return home a hero in the process?*

The dismal procession had passed right by me while I was reflecting on the past couple weeks. I knew there were two officers and a chaplain, then two prisoners and twenty privates with guns. I didn't look very closely at any of them, as I was trying to divorce myself from the whole event. There had been some talk, back and forth, which I refused to pay close attention to. One of the prisoners was given a drink from a canteen, and then they were taken to their stakes and blindfolded.

"Attention," came the order to the twenty men who'd been selected to perform the execution. "Load nine times. Load!" The soldiers brought their muskets in front of them and there was a roaring in my ears.

Tom had already told me that these men had been court-martialed for cowardice. What chance did I have of standing up bravely to what these men apparently couldn't face?

I focused hard on the neck of the man in front of me with my brain working to figure out the best way to get out of the army I'd worked so hard to get in.

When the command to fire was finally given, I couldn't block out the sharp bark of the muskets as they were discharged. I had to go home—there was no way I could pull this charade off once we went into battle.

The answer was surprisingly simple. I would just go to General George Thomas and tell him the truth. Then he'd send me home. Or he would send me to prison. Prison or the battlefield? Which would I be able to handle better? Were those my choices? It was hard to know since I was not sure how General Thomas would react to a female in the ranks of "his men." General Thomas would send me home; I had to believe it because I was sure I couldn't face a battle.

After we'd been dismissed, Tom came up to me and patted my shoulder, "You okay, kid?"

"I'm not sure," I said weakly. "I don't think I can do this soldier thing." I didn't like how desperate my voice sounded to my own ears.

"You'll be fine, kid. Just stick with old Tom and I'll keep you out of trouble." I gave him a weak and surely grim smile, thinking that I had made the right decision to reveal my identity. Then Tom interrupted my thoughts by saying, "Guess what, kid? I found out who can help you find your big brother."

Tom was clearly trying to distract me from what I'd seen that morning and I was grateful to him, especially since it must have been worse for him to watch since he'd known one of the men executed.

The truth was Tom didn't believe I'd ever find Johnny. After listening to me asking questions for the hundredth time, he'd finally said, with some irritation, "Look kid, your brother is either dead or in prison up North. There isn't a thing you can do for him here, so forget it."

Now I grasped at the distraction he'd offered me and asked, "Who? Who did you find that could help me find my brother?"

"Well, it appears he had a buddy who almost always fought next to him by the name of Rob Cody." I gasped. Of course, I should have asked about Cody immediately. My eagerness melted quickly as I realized Cody would likely know for a certainty that Johnny only had a younger sister, no younger brothers.

But, I'd just trimmed my hair again that morning, and I was filthy—there was no way he'd look at me and see a girl. I could tell Cody that Johnny and I were so different in ages that he'd probably never mentioned me. I could act hurt and surprised that he didn't know who I was.

Whatever I told him it wouldn't matter because he probably knew where Johnny was right now, and I needed something positive to hold on to.

"Can you take me to him?" I asked Tom, jumping up off the ground where I'd plopped and just barely remembering not to throw my arms around him in a very female reaction.

"Come on, kid, let's go find him."

I stopped, "Wait a minute. I thought you told me to give this up. Why are you helping me?"

Tom's grin was a little sheepish. "I still think you should give it up," he admitted. "There's nothing you can do for your brother. But I guess you remind me a little of my own kids at home. I help them, even when it is useless. Since I can't help them now, I guess I'll help you."

"Thank you, Tom," I said sincerely. He brushed it off and started walking away. I had to jog to catch up with him.

We wound through the camp, avoiding poker games and a spur-of-the-moment prayer meeting. We passed men eating, trying to repair their clothes or their shoes, and some who were writing letters. As we came near a group of men from the 35th sitting down, probably talking about the events of the morning, one broke off midsentence and stood with a grin.

"Tommyboy, what are you doing clear over here on our side of the camp?" he asked boisterously while pumping Tom's hand and slapping his back.

Tom laughed, "Don't you boy me you young scoundrel. I brought someone to meet you—brother of a friend of yours. Robby, this is Samuel Davis."

Cody suddenly became serious and two deep blue questioning eyes were turned on me. "Samuel Davis, hey?" As the handsome blond looked at me, my mouth went dry.

He knows, I thought in panic, *I haven't even said anything and he knows.*

"That's right," said Tom. "He's Johnny Davis's little brother, Sam's been askin' around to see if anyone knows what might have happened to Johnny. I guess you'd know better than anyone."

One of Rob Cody's blond brows raised as he said, "Sam Davis, Johnny's little *brother?*" Was it my imagination or did he place the slightest emphasis on the word *brother?*

I thought I'd been so clever by using the name Samuel, knowing that when people called me Sam I'd remember to answer. Johnny was the only one at home who shortened my name. He used to love to see Mother's reaction when he called me Sammie Annie.

Now, I could see too clearly the error of my ways. If Johnny called me Sammie Annie to my face, he would certainly call me that when talking to his friends. I had not been in the army long, but already I was gathering bits of information about the families of the soldiers in my mess—those I ate with regularly—and the soldiers in my regiment.

I could see Tom and Rob Cody were both awaiting my answer to Rob's question, and it was too late to change my "name" now. Besides, I still wasn't convinced I wanted to stay in this army so I simply said, "That's right. My brother, Johnny, was listed as Missing in Action after the battle at Gettysburg. I hope some day to find him."

Tom interjected, "I've told him he might as well forget it. Johnny Davis is either dead or in a Yankee prison."

I saw the flash of pain on Rob's face and was sure it mirrored my own. Rob's voice was steady though when he said, "Likely you're right, Tom. We lost a lot of men in that battle."

His expression had gone blank, like he was trying to distance himself from some horrible memories. Looking me full in the face again, but still with shuttered eyes, he said, "Johnny will find his way home if he is alive."

"I know," I answered, "but if he is wounded, I might need to help him get home. Besides that, Father and Mother need to know either way. Johnny was..." I hesitated, not knowing what to say, and then finally had to settle for, "...special. Yes, he was special to all of us and we need to know."

Tom entered the conversation again. "What you need to know, kid, is how to keep your gun clean and your head down, or some brother is going to do some fool thing like join the army to find you."

I absently responded, "There is no one left to come find me."

Again, Rob Cody's brow winged up in surprised question. Tom said, "There you go then. Forget your brother's whereabouts and come back to get ready for parade."

Disappointed that Johnny's good friend agreed with Tom, I started to follow Tom back to camp. "Sam!" Rob called, and I stopped to hear what he had to say. He hesitated and then just said, "Maybe I'll see you around some time." For some reason, I was sure that was not what he'd been intending to say, but it was time to get ready for our evening parade.

TWO

Orange County Court House
September 1863

The next weeks I fell into the routine of camp life, deciding that until I could get information from Rob Cody I would not reveal myself to General Thomas. Reveille, roll call, and drills in the morning, parade in the afternoon, and eating with a group of five other men, called a "mess." Then there were huge blocks of down time in the middle of the day.

Many of the men had taken to religion, and there were prayer meetings and revivals going on all the time. Poker games also were going on all the time and playing practical jokes helped to relieve the endless monotony.

In many ways, being the butt of a practical joke was an indication of acceptance, or a way to test reactions when battle wasn't raging so that your comrades would know if you could be trusted in a difficult situation. When the mess played a joke on me, I knew that I was finally one of the guys. It was not because they played the joke, but more because from their reactions I knew I'd handled it well.

Hunger was becoming a constant companion, though to hear the veterans tell it, we had more food available at camp than usual. Looking at the way their bones stood out, it was easy to believe that the food supply in camp was more regular than it had been in the past. Supply wagons did come fairly regularly, but there were a lot of men to feed.

Two of the mess groups were eating together that night as a couple of men (one from each mess) had "acquired" two fresh chickens. It was my night to cook for our mess, and since I was the recruit it fell to me to cook for both messes. I didn't mind but couldn't help feeling badly for the men who would be eating my chickens. Cooking never was one of the things I did well. At home we had Hettie to cook, so camp was my first real experience with food preparation.

I plucked the chickens clean and gutted them, and then I placed them over the fire to cook. I started to get some cornmeal bread mixed and got called away for just a minute. When I came back, I checked on the chickens and found to my surprise there was nothing on the spit over the fire where I'd left the chickens. I knew that no one in either mess would just get rid of good fresh meat, even for a practical joke, so I looked around for the chickens.

Having found them in a pan simmering under the ashes of the fire and cooking quite well, I left the pan there and went back to fixing the cornbread.

The men of the two messes gathered for the meal with their odd assortment of plates and utensils. I pulled the spit off the fire and pretended to be shocked with surprise. Then I shrugged my shoulders in an exaggerated fashion and started dishing up the feathers I had put aside after plucking the chickens saying, "I guess this is the only chicken we have." The looks on the men's faces as they were given a plate of feathers ranged from shock and disbelief to barely concealed laughter.

Mac sneered at me and said, "Look at this Johnny Raw, don't even know what part of a chicken ta cook."

"Oh, to hear ya'll talk, I thought this is how all you veterans liked your chicken. I'm too much of a Johnny Raw to be ready to eat chicken feathers just yet. I'm going to eat the meat." I pulled the other pan out of the ashes with a flourish.

Everyone laughed at me and then started slapping me on the back. Someone said, "You take a joke real good, boy." We got rid of the feathers and everyone enjoyed their meal of tender chicken meat with the usual weevil-infested cornbread.

Some of the pranks were not as innocent and could have disastrous results. Often these were done out of spite by people who disliked you or wanted to teach you a lesson. I, also, was subjected to one of these more unkind pranks while I was on guard duty the first time.

The first night I had picket duty, I was nervous. Picket duty involved guarding the outer limits of the camp while the other soldiers slept. We were watching for spies and surprise attacks by the Yankees. Granted, the Yankees were not close, to our knowledge, but picket duty was important. That made it stressful for those of us who'd never done it before.

Tom had warned me to watch my back during picket duty. He told me stories about other recruits who'd been foolish enough to fire on fellow Confederates when they went out on picket for the first time. Results had ranged from a good laugh to court-martial. Having noticed the way Mac had been tormenting me, Tom guessed the situation would be pushed as far as Mac would take it.

"I'm not saying anyone will bother you tonight," Tom said. "Just be on your guard for idiots as well as Yanks." Then he stood up and left the fire.

Mac added to the nerves I was feeling that night by trying to betray me into falsely sounding an alarm to warn the camp of Yankees nearby. A false alarm would mean discipline from the commanding officers. The night was well advanced and the whole camp seemed to be asleep. Out of nowhere, I started hearing noises like someone was creeping up to me. Remembering Tom's warning, I started listening harder to determine where the noises were coming from.

After straining to listen for some time, I felt like I'd pinpointed the location as slightly behind me and to the left. Behind me? If this was a real Yankee emergency, they certainly wouldn't be coming from inside the camp.

As the noises moved closer, I put the butt of my rifle on the ground and casually started to whistle. Johnny had taught me how (much to my mother's frustration), and the skill had served me well in the army, as ladies of the South do not whistle.

I kept careful track of the progress of the person creeping up on me. He was near now; I turned a little to my left and scanned the area. I saw a shadow move while crouching near the ground. The person took a position like he was getting ready to spring on me. I thought the plan must be to tackle me so he wouldn't get hurt by a stray shot. He tensed and I tensed, and then he sprang with a yell and I lunged to the side. I recognized Mac after he'd caught nothing but a face full of dirt. I squatted down beside his prone body and said in a friendly tone, "Hey Mac. Did you come to keep me company on picket duty?" Mac growled, and then the sergeant responsible for the pickets that night ran over to find out what the yelling was about.

I quickly stood up and said, "Nothing sir, just a joke by some of my mess mates. I'm sorry to alarm anyone." The truth was, no one except the sergeant had heard Mac yell. It seemed loud in the silence, but it was little more than a grunt—just enough to startle me.

"Return to your duty," the sergeant snapped. Mac just glowered at me, his resentment clear and stronger than before, as he went back to his guard duty on the picket line.

☙

I came to realize in those first weeks in camp that finding Johnny would be nothing short of a miracle. I'd asked around to see what others remembered about the last time they'd seen my brother. Some of them remembered seeing him in his last known battle at Gettysburg. But if they would talk about it—and very few of them would—it seemed there had been so much confusion and smoke that any information I could gather contradicted what I'd heard from someone else.

Rob Cody was the most difficult to pin down. While he was always kind to me, he never gave me any hope that he had any opinion other than that Johnny was taken prisoner or was dead.

I came to the conclusion that there was little point in trying to find Johnny by piecing together his last days of battle. And even if I could find some answers, there was always the question of what I would do with the information.

Tom had told me that I wouldn't be granted furlough to go find my long lost brother once I determined where he might be. After all, there was still a war going on even if the only action we had seen since I had joined up was long (usually wet and cold) marches. Furloughs were not given often, even less often now than before Gettysburg, as the need for manpower in the Confederate States of America seemed to always be greater than the actual manpower available for our army.

I started asking fewer, but more important questions about my brother, and I started finding my own rhythm at the camp. By this time I was determined to stay. Having been accepted by the soldiers, I didn't want to let down my new brothers.

I stayed away from Mac and the others who were like him and spent more time in the company of Tom and Rob Cody, finding in each of them a friend. Tom watched over me, and I was always more comfortable with him. I knew his interest in me was because of the connection he felt for his sons back home. Tom informed me he'd take a birch switch to any of his sons for joining up since they were all underage. He clearly thought that I was very nearly the same age as his oldest, who was about fourteen, and I let him continue in that belief.

I enjoyed being with Rob more than Tom, but I always had to be careful in Rob's company. I constantly tried to determine how much he knew about our family and if he could possibly know I was a girl.

Regarding my relatives in the 35th, I simply avoided them at all possible cost. I wasn't sure how they would react to me being in the army, and I felt the best way to keep everyone happy was just to leave them in complete ignorance of my decision. I was camping within half a mile of their campsite. I probably could have left them ignorant of my existence in their camp for months if Rob Cody hadn't forced me to confront them.

THREE

~

Orange County Court House
October 1863

"*You do that a whole lot better than Johnny ever did,*" the lazy voice interrupted me as I bit off the thread at the end of a stitch. Glancing up from where I sat on the ground crosslegged (and wasn't it glorious to sit crosslegged) darning a sock, I saw Robert Cody. His arms crossed his chest as he leaned nonchalantly against a young tree that had escaped the firewood-seeking hatchets because it was too green.

I felt myself flush and wondered how long he'd been standing there watching me sew. I knew the men usually had to repair their own clothing. Still, I hoped I'd done nothing to give myself away. Rob went on, smiling, "Every time Johnny tried to darn a pair of socks, they ended up puckered so badly he could hardly get a shoe on over the repair."

"Well, I may be able to darn a sock better than my brother, but I'm sure I don't cook half as good as he does," I said grinning back at Rob.

"Boy isn't that the truth," muttered Tom who was sitting at the base of the green sapling. Tom was smoking his pipe and reading a newspaper he'd just gotten in the mail call that afternoon. The paper was only four months old and therefore required his immediate attention. This afternoon was perfect for reading since the sun had finally come out the day before, and we were all basking in its warmth after our drills and parade.

I gave Tom a mock scowl and said, "You're not required to eat what I cook. You could always take my day for me."

"Judging from the holes in your pants, you cook better than you sew, too," Rob laughed at Tom.

Tom muttered something that I didn't catch and started puffing on his pipe again.

"You know, Tom, you're the only one in our mess who I've seen let the holes get bigger and bigger without even trying to do a thing about it," I said, struck by that observation.

"Why don't you work a trade?" asked Rob. "Sam will patch for you if you cook for him."

Hating to cook, I jumped on that suggestion double quick, "Yeah, Tom. Then you don't have to eat my cooking, and you don't have to go around in breezy britches."

Tom glared at me and said, "Listen to you making it sound like a big favor to me. You hate to cook over that fire and we all know it."

"True, but it would still be a good deal."

"All right, I'll cook your next turn if you patch up the knees of my pants," Tom said trying to sound grumpy.

I immediately said, "You have two knees that need patched up, that will cost you two meals."

Seeing Tom was about to growl again, Rob said, "It's only fair—a patch a meal."

"Fine," said Tom. "I'll do your next two turns at mess if you patch up the knees of my pants."

"Great," I said smiling at him. "Then I don't have to eat my cooking either."

Tom started laughing and Rob grabbed my hand and pulled me to my feet saying impatiently, "Come on, Samuel, I'm taking you to see someone."

Was it my imagination, or did he emphasize my name? And what made him cross about the deal he'd just helped me work with Tom?

"Where are we going?" I asked as I rushed to keep up with his long strides. After pulling me up from my sitting position, he'd stuffed his hands in his pockets and strode off, knowing I'd follow.

"Just to see some folks I'm sure you'd like to see," he answered evasively.

"Who?" I asked.

"How long you been here, Sam?" He asked instead of answering me.

"Six weeks or so."

"In six weeks you've been asking around about your brother, making me crazy with all your questions. You've figured out how to go on so the sergeant doesn't bark at you anymore. You've even got Mac to lay off some."

"So?" I was clearly missing the point.

"It just seems that in six weeks you would have looked for and found some familiar faces. But it seems to me you're avoiding them."

I stopped in my tracks and felt the blood drain from my face. "What do you mean?" I didn't like the panicked note I heard in my voice.

Rob stopped and faced me. "I think you know. Johnny was in my company, which was odd since we mustered from a different county. But he couldn't leave when the folks from your area mustered, right? He followed a couple of weeks later and that is why he ended up with us, because the company with your neighbors and your uncle and your cousins had a full roster by the time he got there."

"So, what does that have to do with me?"

Rob grabbed my elbow and pulled me along with him. "It just seems odd to me that you as a new recruit—especially with the way Mac has been treating you—wouldn't seek out a familiar face or two for support."

"Listen," I said, in a real panic now, "I don't think this is a good idea."

It was too late. Rob took a couple of steps so he was in front of me. I couldn't see whom he was talking to, but I heard his words clearly enough. "Hey Davis, guess who I found fighting with the 14th?"

Unmistakably, I heard my uncle's voice. "Hey Cody, been a while since I shot the breeze with you. Who'd you find?"

Dragging me forward, he said, "Why, I brought you *Samuel Davis*, your *nephew*." There was no mistaking the emphasis he put on my name this time. He also stressed the word *nephew*, but I had barely taken this in when I saw my Uncle Frank. He was thinner than I had ever seen him, surprisingly there was a look of relief on his face.

I noted that all movement stopped when Cody thrust me into the center of their group, but I only had shocked and pleading eyes for my uncle.

After studying the changes in me for a long, intense moment, Uncle Frank smiled and threw his arm around me. He slapped my back roughly, just as if I was his nephew instead of his niece. "Well, Sammie, why didn't you tell us you'd joined up?"

"Look who joined up, boys!" Uncle Frank said loudly to the men nearby. Cousins and neighbors from home instantly surrounded me. I was slapped on my back, and lots of questions and comments were shouted at me.

My cousin Charles even put me in a headlock, dislodging my cap as he roughly ran his knuckles back and forth over my head. It was the way he always greeted my brother.

No one said anything to betray my secret, but I saw the look of blank bewilderment on the face of my neighbor,

George Smythe. There was also scorn on the face of my cousin James.

After the rowdy greeting by my kin and neighbors, we settled down so I could give an account to everyone of their own family, all the things that hadn't been put in letters. Rob Cody stayed, settling in and listening to me answer questions about Aunt Fran and her girls at home, how they were managing the farm, and how they spent hours and hours every week taking care of the less fortunate in our community. The less fortunate were those who had lost their men because of the war. She always made sure the children were fed, and she sent the family's servants to help the people who were really struggling and trying to get crops in during this difficult war.

Charles wanted to hear about the young wife he'd left behind and the daughter who had been born after his last furlough. George Smythe asked about how his mother and sister were bearing up since hearing that his father had died during the war.

The conversation turned naturally to memories of past days, and there was a lot of laughter even if it was touched with a bit of wistfulness. Finally, having patiently listened for an hour about people he didn't know, Rob said, "Come on Sam, I'll take you back. Tom will be wondering where you are so you can fix his pants."

George scowled and James sneered. When Uncle Frank said he'd walk with us, Rob didn't offer any resistance.

When we were out of sight of Uncle Frank's camping area, I said, "Uncle Frank, you didn't seem too surprised to see me."

He shrugged and said, "Why should I be? The fact that you have no business being somewhere never stopped you from getting into trouble before."

"Why doesn't he have any business being here?" Rob asked a little bit too casually.

Uncle Frank flushed a little and, glancing at Rob and then at me, said, "It's obvious to anyone who looks at the lad he's too young to fight in this war. He doesn't even have the shadow of a whisker on his baby face." Rob laughed and I flushed.

Then Uncle Frank continued, "Your father had letters written to me twice since July. The first time with some foolish idea about finding Johnny by piecing together where he'd been during his last battle. By the time my letter got to him, I guess you'd already taken off because his next letter came telling me to watch out for you. I told the boys to be on the lookout for you, warned them not to make a big fuss about you..." He cast a glance at Rob Cody and then continued, "...age. Your Father said you had been trying to find out whatever happened to Johnny, him being missing and all."

I said, "That's right. We only heard that he'd been in that big battle at Gettysburg, and then that he wasn't counted among the living, dead, or wounded. He can't have just disappeared."

Uncle Frank nodded, "True, but we'll probably never know what happened to him. Battles are a noisy, confusing, bloody mess. Lots of soldiers go missing during a battle—and I don't mean because they run away," Uncle Frank added hastily when he saw my defensive look.

"You been in a real battle yet, Sammie?" When I shook my head, he gave a knowing and very bleak smile and said, "Well, when you've seen one, you'll know just how easy it is to lose track of a man in a battle."

"But..."

Uncle Frank shook his head and said, "It's a fool thing you've done. We aren't going to find Johnny this way."

"Father thought that if we could just get close enough to the men who were fighting with him and ask them the last time they remembered seeing him, we might be able to piece the thing together and find him."

Uncle Frank snorted and said bitterly, "How very like your father to think you could come and get some information and then coldly figure where Johnny was likely to be. The messy, hot-blooded truth of the fight wouldn't even enter into his mind. Like once we thought back on that smoky, smelly mess we'd be able to say, 'Well, now that you ask, I remember seeing Johnny help a fallen brother off the field of combat at quarter after twelve as I was taking a drink of water out of my canteen.' Tell me, did he put you up to joining?"

"No," I said, flushing. "I ran off and joined by myself. Father and Mother were discussing it and I knew the army wouldn't ever take Father because of his hand.

Besides, Mother would have been unbearable if Father had gone off. So, being younger and healthy, I joined instead of him."

Nodding, Uncle Frank said, "Well, Sammie, Johnny isn't here and you're going to have to live with the consequences of your decision. Hope you don't regret it, but me and the boys won't see you kicked out"—glancing again at Rob he added with great emphasis—"because of your age. The Davis family finishes what we start, and much as you'll come to hate starting this adventure, you'll finish it."

"But I'm sure I could find Johnny with..."

Surprisingly, Rob Cody was the one who interrupted saying flatly, "Sam, leave it alone. No one wants to go back and relive battles—especially that one, especially as concerns Johnny."

I looked at him and saw that his face was blank, and his blue eyes that always seemed to be filled with amusement now seemed exceedingly bleak. I suddenly realized that both men walking beside me were sure Johnny was dead, and that they missed him nearly as much as I did.

I refused to believe Johnny could be dead, and I decided to leave these men in peace about it. I'd already determined the futility of trying to find Johnny this way.

"Okay, I'll leave it alone," I muttered.

Uncle Frank slapped my back and told me I was a good *boy*. As we were nearly at my campsite, he told me he'd be heading back to his own fire. He then turned and left us.

FOUR

Bristoe Station, Virginia
October 1863

The rain was cold and constant. We stood waiting for our turn to join the fighting going on ahead and got soaked in the chilling rain. The sound of fired cannon balls echoed all around us. Occasionally, the sulfur smell of the smoke wafted back to us as we stood in reserve, waiting for the time when our officers would determine our brigade was needed up front.

I was exhausted, not from my first forced march, but from the tension of waiting for what would likely be my first battle. It sounded so heroic and noble at the beginning of the war when our boys first marched away. Years at home made the idea of battle more worrisome, especially when the casualty lists started being printed.

Now, as I stood at the edge of the formation of my brigade, the horror of battle was taking on a whole new reality. Since joining the army, my first battle had loomed before me—an obstacle I had to overcome to prove myself to those in my regiment. It was an obstacle I had to overcome to prove myself to me as well.

Grim determination had gripped me from the start. When I thought of battle, that determination had only intensified with Mac's taunts, Tom's kindness, and Rob's tentative friendship. I had steeled myself to face the noise and the guns, knowing deep down I could handle the fight. I had to, since I'd chosen this road to finding my brother.

That resolve had not been shaken with the first deafening volley of artillery, or the echoes of the rebel yell that we could hear from our position well behind the front lines. I had not been truly shaken until the first of the bloody and broken bodies had limped up the road past us to the field hospital set up to our rear.

For hours now, that dragged on like soggy days, the wounded had come past our waiting regiment. Some limped by, using their muskets as crutches; wounded comrades supported others. Many more were carried past on stretchers, and the stretcher bearers grimly passed back and forth before our watchful regiment.

Sometimes, the surgeon's assistant would be giving immediate first aid as he walked next to the stretcher. He did whatever he could to keep the wounded soldier alive until they got to the field hospital. This was the scenario when I was pulled to help.

I had noticed the stretcher bearers because they had passed our position several times already that morning. I also noticed the soldier at one end of the stretcher was not the same bearer who had previously passed going toward the field. Walking between the stretcher and my regiment was a surgeon's assistant trying to stop some bleeding as the soldier on the stretcher lay motionless.

The solider who was holding the second end of the stretcher seemed to be holding himself up by sheer willpower. He stumbled and slipped in the mud, but he continued.

When the injured and his assistants got to where I was standing, the soldier stumbled again. He then fell to his knees, offsetting the balance of the stretcher. The surgeon's assistant said something sharply, and then he glanced at the soldier and saw the same thing I had just noticed. There was a spreading red stain on the upper chest of his butternut-colored uniform.

The surgeon's assistant snapped at me and the soldier in front of me (who, as luck would have it, happened to be Mac) to get over there and help.

A surgeon's orders—even a surgeon's assistant—trumped almost everyone's orders, so Mac and I rushed to help. Mac took one end of the stretcher, leaving me with the soldier who was now semiconscious and lying in the muddy road.

Kneeling beside him, I lifted him to his knees and worked my shoulders under his right arm and wrapped my left arm around his waist. I was extremely grateful that he was not much taller than I and that he wasn't very heavy as I dragged him back to the hospital area.

By the time I arrived with my charge, Mac was knee-deep in helping move men into the hospital tent. As he hauled another man into the tent, the surgeon's assistant who recruited me snapped out, "Stop his bleeding as best you can! I'll be back for him in a minute." I eased my burden to the wet ground and knelt beside him, digging in my knapsack for the field dressings we were required to carry with us at all times. Having located the bandages, I bent over the young man. I could see he was probably younger than I, and I started working the buttons of his uniform blouse so I could find his wound and try to stop the bleeding.

His eyes opened suddenly and he reached up and grasped my hands weakly. "No," he croaked out in barely a whisper.

"Hush now, I'm going to stop the bleeding. Then we'll get you in to the surgeon. You're going to be fine." I kept reassuring him as I worked the buttons on his wet and filthy uniform.

Laboriously, gasping between every word, he said, "No…I'm…a…good…soldier."

I responded soothingly, "One of the best." I was finally able to yank his shirt open and look for his wound. Stunned, I paused as I saw a piece of cloth exactly like the one I wore under my own tunic to ensure that no one would guess I was a girl. My eyes flew to her face.

With dim eyes she was watching my reaction, "Don't... tell...I'm...a...good...soldier."

"One of the best," I repeated. Looking at her face, this time I said, "Your secret is safe with me."

She sighed audibly, her eyes rolled up into her head, and her whole body relaxed. While she breathed shallowly, I rebuttoned her tunic. By the time I had wrestled the last button into its wet buttonhole, her shallow breathing had stopped.

The surgeon's assistant came to get her. One glance told him she was gone so he said, "Take the body over there." He pointed to a pile of other bodies out of the way of the wounded. "We'll have him buried with the rest of them later! Then come and help over here."

I went behind her, and wrapping my arms around her, I dragged her to the place the surgeon's assistant had indicated. With a heavy heart, I left her to be buried in the mass grave that would be dug later that night and went to help with the wounded.

It was a grisly afternoon, and I spent much of it dragging the dead away from the wounded to make room for more wounded, who just kept coming. I preferred that job though, as unhappy as it made me to have to face the death of so many men, to trying to ease the pain of those who were not able to find the release of death.

The moans and cries of those wounded I knew would haunt me my whole life. But even that was better than the screams and shrieks that came from the tent where limbs beyond any hope of saving were being sawed off.

After hearing one of these poor victims screaming, Mac grabbed the feet of the corpse I was moving out of the way. Gruffly he said, "They are doin' the only thing they can. If they left 'em be, it'd get infected, kill 'em slowly an' with lots of pain."

Equally as gruffly I answered, "I know."

I could tell that I wasn't completely convincing because Mac said, "They be outta whiskey ta kill the pain."

Nodding I turned to go back to the wounded. Finally, as the sun was slipping down to the edge of the sky, I was told to go back to my unit as the orderlies could handle it from there. I bolted without waiting to see if Mac had also been released or if the slowing of wounded only provided a reprieve for me.

Halfway back to our regiment, I couldn't hold on anymore and I slipped off into the woods on the side of the road. I stumbled through the first undergrowth before collapsing over a log and becoming violently sick to my stomach.

As I finished heaving, I sensed a presence beside me. Slowly turning I found Mac sitting not too far away, puffing on his pipe and looking the other way in great concentration. As if realizing I knew he was there, he silently handed me his canteen without looking at me. Gratefully, I took it and rinsed my mouth several times before finally taking a long swallow.

After several long seconds of silence, Mac asked, "Ya gonna be okay, kid?"

Bitterly I said, "You're right Mac. I'm just a baby who shouldn't be here—now you're all at risk because you'll be babysitting me."

Taking his canteen from my hand, Mac took a long drink and then looked me squarely in the eye. "Ya proved today ya got the spine ta be a good soldier. I ain't worried 'bout goin' to battle with ya."

I started to protest when he said, "Look kid, most folk don' ever have ta deal with all the stuff ya dealt with today. Ya'll fight all the harder ta keep away from the sawbones, an' ya waited 'til ya had done all ya needed ta before ya lost yer lunch. Ya did good today, kid."

Heartened by Mac's gruff approval, I nodded and got shakily to my feet. "I guess we'd better get back."

"Yep," Mac said. "Hope the others have already dug in. It's gonna be a cold one tonight."

It didn't take us long to get back to the 14th, and they had already "dug in," which I learned meant digging the trenches we'd be fighting from the next day.

Despite my grim day and the pounding rain, I couldn't help but smile as I drifted off to sleep that night. I was thinking about how my father and mother would react if they could see their baby girl now.

I was drenched to the bone from the incessant cold rain, not to mention covered with mud and whatever else had smeared on me while I was helping the wounded. Johnny's old floppy hat was pulled over my face to protect it from the rain and my pillow was my lumpy knapsack.

With no thought of what was proper and every thought of getting as much heat as I could from my comrades, I was huddled as closely as possible to the men in my company—snuggled between Tom and Mac.

I'd come a long way from the little girl whom my mother scolded for dirty and often ripped pinafores. Then again, maybe I hadn't come that far at all. After all, the little girl in the dirty pinafore had done only what the girl in the dirty butternut wool uniform was doing—following in the footsteps of her favorite sibling, Johnny Davis.

It was very likely that I'd follow his footsteps right into a battle with the Yankees the next day.

FIVE

Orange County Court House and Shenandoah Valley
November-December 1863

As it turned out, I didn't have to prove myself in battle the following day, or even the one after that. We dug in and shifted position and dug in again. The rain continued to fall, and we continued to huddle together every night for a little bit of warmth. We ate stale hardtack full of bugs. The supply wagons, which carried all our blankets and food and cooking supplies, couldn't get through the bog the roads had become.

Finally, the order came—we were to attack the Yankee position the following morning. I was sick with nerves and, to my shame, excitement.

The morning came and even then I didn't fight in my first real battle because the Yankees crept away in the night. Truth to tell, we were just as happy not to have to engage. We'd heard the Yankee force we would have been up against was quite a bit larger than the couple of regiments that comprised our current camp.

We marched back to the camp at Orange County Court House and prepared to settle in for winter. This march and wait, however, had a larger effect on the men in my brigade than I had realized while we were there.

Rumors started flying about the number of soldiers in the Union army, the number of muskets, and even the number of foreign recruits the Union was pulling in each month.

Jim Fletcher and Jake Edwards, veterans in our company, were sitting with us one night. Fletcher said, "Edwards says the Yanks are getting 10,000 foreigners to fight for 'em each month."

Tom snorted and answered, "Edwards, you're a fool. There probably aren't 10,000 foreigners in the whole country—much less the Union army."

"Even if there ain't that many, the Yanks still got all the men they could need. We gotta force people to fight for us," Fletcher replied.

"What are you trying to say, boy?" Tom asked.

"Nothin'," was the grunted reply. "I'm jus' tired of always bein' on the short end is all."

It was clear to everyone that Fletcher was sure we had no hope of ever winning this war. The last fight we'd witnessed seemed to show us just how ugly the odds were.

It had been discouraging to watch the wounded limping back behind the lines to the hospital. We knew we were the only brigade available to come to the rescue. Then we lost the opportunity to even try to fight the five Union brigades we heard we'd been sent to face.

When I told Rob Cody about Fletcher's comments, he said, "It doesn't do any good to worry about it. However it ends and whenever it ends, we have a job to do until that day or until we can't do the job anymore."

Looking into his bleak and weary face, I asked, "Are you tired of it? The fighting I mean."

"Sure I am. I'd be surprised if you could find anyone who'd been here any length of time who wasn't tired of it." He responded with a shrug and then started talking about other things.

The troops were discouraged, but as everyone started building more permanent structures to spend the winter in, the mood seemed to lighten. It was amusing, yet sad, for me to watch the men work on their shanties and try to add touches to make their living space home. The little log shacks that we built were useful to keep the worst of the frost and rain out. The men did their best to make these little dwellings more homelike with things sent in packages from loved ones. Some men even went so far as to build makeshift fireplaces in their huts. There was lots of discussion about the best way to build a structure, which was a relief since earlier the discussions had been about whether to build at all.

In October, there was no consensus as to whether we were done chasing Yanks for the season. Rumors had been ripe about us heading west into the Shenandoah Valley to help General Early's troops. Tom had said at the time, "Heaven knows those boys in the west could use our help."

Mac agreed, "I think we ain't stayin' here long, so I ain't willin' ta put up anythin' more permanent. We got those little Yank tents ta keep us some dry. They'll have ta do fer now."

Now, however, we were headed into December, and everyone seemed to think it was time for something warmer. I hooked up with Tom, Mac, and Steve Jones (who joined up the same time I did). We built a little shelter that, while not tight enough to keep the wind out, at least gave us a roof and a chimney to help keep the rain out and the fire's warmth in.

When we first started building our shelter, I wondered if Mac would want to spend his time with two recruits, as he'd shown no interest in any of us before. Then I realized that Mac's contempt for the recruits had never really included Steve, even in the beginning. That probably was because he came from the same part of Georgia Mac hailed from.

After the conversation Mac and I had when we'd been helping the wounded, Mac was showing me a lot more respect. Edwards and Fletcher were the other two men we regularly ate with, and the six of us made up our mess. Ever since coming back from our latest engagement, these two seemed to be getting on Mac's last nerve with their gloomy outlook and pessimistic ideas on where our army was going (defeat and fast).

Even the ever-patient Tom was losing patience rapidly with Edwards and Fletcher. I realized it was little wonder Mac would prefer to spend the winter with the three of us rather than finding a place in a whole new mess.

A lot of the men started applying for furlough—as no one wanted to be in our little shantytown at Christmas time. The supply wagons were not getting through, and we were all hungry and cold. Men were writing their families, asking them to send food and warmer clothes.

☙

We were all looking forward to a lonely and quiet winter, when in mid-December orders had us packing our gear again and getting ready to march. There was much complaining and swearing among the rank and file, and even the officers appeared none too pleased about leaving their "cabins" for long and cold marches where food was sure to be even scarcer than it was at camp.

Despite all the grumbling, we were ready to go in good order and on our way to the train station in Alexandria. We had to wait most of the day in the cold before we were loaded into boxcars and headed, via Gordonsville, to the Shenandoah Valley.

It was in the Shenandoah Valley where I learned how cold snow could really be and how rain could freeze as it touched the ground. The first morning as we got out of the boxcars, I caught my breath when I saw how pretty everything looked coated in the frozen rain.

By that night I was hating it as the freezing rain turned to sleet and then driving snow, and we had no wood to feed the fires. Finally, in total desperation, Mac went to a nearby farm with a group from the regiment. They pulled the fences apart to put on the fire, even though the wood was wet.

We'd been sent to the Shenandoah Valley to help General Early's brigade stop Union Cavalry and infantry, which we missed completely as they took a route different from the one expected by our leaders. "Don't worry though—the fun isn't over," Tom said.

He informed us the rumor mill had started grinding again. "Word is that there is another regiment over near Harrisonburg where we will go and convince those Yankees to leave our fair Valley." Sure enough, that same day we were ordered to march again— this time toward Harrisonburg.

The Federal troops didn't oblige us by waiting for us to arrive, so we began marching again in hot pursuit. The march was more than miserable with the cold seeping into our bones. I was one of the few lucky ones on the march, probably because I was still so new. I had shoes. Whenever I thought I couldn't go on, I'd watch a comrade limp along in the snow barefooted and realize I had nothing to complain about.

The other thing that helped was Tom's amazing baritone voice. He seemed to know just when we were drooping to the point of not being able to continue when he'd break into a stirring version of "Dixie," "The Bonnie Blue Flag," or some fun and rollicking ditty.

Before too long, the music would travel up and down the line of tramping soldiers, and all the shoulders that had started to slump would suddenly straighten again. The feet that had started to drag along the ground would again lift with painful purpose.

One very memorable and great day, we awoke to a foot and a half of snow. The half-expected order to march did not come, and it wasn't long before we had a major snowball fight in progress. It was complete with battle plans and prisoners of war.

The battle was a novel experience for those of us from Georgia, where that much snow rarely fell. It also was a great outlet for everyone. We were tired of chasing the Yanks with no results. Naturally, I joined the snowball fight with great enthusiasm, especially since I found myself and my messmates fighting my relatives and Rob Cody.

Two snowforts had been constructed facing one another, behind which most of us took shelter and lobbed snowballs with great precision. Often, however, fort raids were conducted in order to grab prisoners from the other team.

Steve Jones led a fort raid, including myself as one of his men. While the others on our team created a diversion of increased snowballs, yells, and targets on our center and left, six of us tore over the top of our fort on the right. We raced across the short stretch between the two forts and climbed over the top of their snowfort, each tackling and taking a prisoner and dragging him back. The plan was that we would be nearly back to our own fort with our prisoners before the rest of their team could stop us or retaliate against us.

I went over the top of the enemy fort and tackled the man in front of me. As we went down, I saw the look of surprise on Rob Cody's face. We hit the ground, but Rob reacted quickly pinning me and rubbing snow in my face. Squirming out from under him, I sat up sputtering and laughing. "I surrender," I said laughing as I protected my face while Rob grabbed another handful of snow.

"Good," he replied, also laughing and climbing to his feet. Rob reached down a hand for me and said, "Now, you go to the holding pen with your comrades." I jumped up without his aid with my own handful of snow, dumping it on his neck so it would ooze down under his shirt and jacket. Then while Rob was trying to shake the snow out of his clothes, I scrambled back over the top of the enemy fort and raced back to my own.

The whole snow battle probably only lasted an hour, but that night there was more laughter and lightheartedness in the camp than there had been since I'd joined. Rob had come over to our fire to congratulate me on surprising him with the snow and getting away from the enemy. I felt a rush of quiet pride that I had impressed him a little.

Tom warned me that if I got caught by Yankees I'd better not do anything that rash, which made be grow a little uneasy. The smile on Rob's face was transformed into grim lines, but after the first little chill I didn't think about being taken prisoner by Yankees. I was more worried about actually fighting them.

The following day, we were marching again.

SIX

Shenandoah Valley
January-March 1864

We marched up and down and then down and up that Valley over the course of the next two months, always in the cold and nearly always hungry. Then, near the end of January, our payroll caught up to us. It was the first time in my life I had earned money that was really my own. My father had not given this money to me, directly or indirectly. What a heady feeling! I knew exactly what I was going to buy first—soap.

I bought it from a camp-following merchant, but I needed a confidant to stand guard while I bathed. I didn't want to be discovered, especially doing such a private thing. I immediately headed over to where the 35th was located and found George Smythe. Sometimes pal, sometimes irritant, he always was my defender from the days before the war.

George had grown up not far from us and was Johnny's friend, and therefore mine as well. Having a much younger sister, and not many cousins around, he spent a lot of time with Johnny. When we were very young, he would tease me mercilessly, until Johnny put a stop to it.

After that it seemed that George didn't like me very much until he came upon my cousin James being slyly mean to me (as James often was). George jumped in and defended me in no uncertain terms, bloodying James' nose and giving him a black eye in the process. George's wounds consisted of a split lip and sore knuckles and one totally devoted little girl, who only preferred her big brother, Johnny, to him.

He put up with me being his shadow with as much grace as Johnny did, until just before the war broke out. We had both grown up enough to be attracted to people of the opposite gender, and then things had gotten awkward. George had continued to defend me as needed, and he stole a quick and surprising kiss before he left with my uncle and cousins to join the army.

Luck was with me and I found George walking by himself toward their fire ring with his arms loaded with wood and whistling tunelessly.

"George, can I talk with you a minute?" I asked, drawing him away from his campsite.

George was clearly surprised; we'd hardly seen each other since the night Rob had brought me to face my

Uncle Frank last October. Predictably he shrugged a little, dumped his wood, and followed me to where I was sure no one would overhear.

"I have a huge favor to ask you," I began. His eyes narrowed and I could tell he was not happy to have me asking a favor of him. I looked at the ground and took a deep breath to calm my suddenly jumping nerves, and then I looked up at him through my lashes. "Would you please stand guard while I take a bath? I haven't had one in ever so long and I am such a fright..."

"Stop it," George interrupted me harshly. My eyes widened in surprise as I looked him full in the face. Angrily, George said, "Don't even try to play that game with me Samantha, especially not here."

"What do you mean?" I asked, bewildered.

"You never batted your lashes at me ever before in our lives. If you didn't try it when you looked all peaches and cream and dressed up for a picnic or something before, don't try it now when you're dressed in butternut trousers with your hair all chopped off in the middle of an army camp."

"I wasn't flirting with you," I whispered stiffly. "Why would I? Someone might see me and figure out I'm a girl. Then who knows whether I'd get sent home or to some prison?"

"Fine," George growled back, "and no, I'm not going to stand guard for you."

"Why not?" I demanded, stunned.

"Because this is a bad idea. What do you want a bath for anyway? It's freezing and you'll be seen and give yourself away."

"I want a bath because I am disgusting and uncomfortable. I want a bath to see if I can get rid of some of these dirty lice and fleas that are driving me crazy. I want a bath because I am the only person in the whole army who can't just go grab one in the river, nor have I been able to clean up in at least two months," I answered. "Besides, no one will see me and I won't be given away if you would just stand guard for a while."

"Well, I won't and that's final," George said grumpily.

"Hey you two," Rob Cody's voice broke into our conversation.

I turned to him and smiled (widely I'm sure) while George turned to him and scowled.

"What's wrong?" Rob asked, "Am I interrupting something?"

"No," George replied a little bit sulkily, "Sam just is trying to talk me into a stupid scheme."

"What is the scheme? Can I join the fun?"

"No," George and I both answered emphatically. At the vehemence of our joint refusal, Rob looked surprised, then amused. I started biting the inside of my lower lip, wondering what I should tell him.

Then George said, "Sam just wants me to come as lookout while she..." I elbowed him sharply. "Uh, he takes a bath. He's shy," George ended lamely.

"I'll stand watch for you," Rob offered. Again both of us shouted, "No."

George said, sulkier still, "I already said I'd do it—no need to bother yourself over little Sammie's shyness."

Rob just shrugged and I changed the subject. Later, with a very grim George standing guard, I had the most wonderful—and cold—bath of my life. I washed my hair four times and also took the time to thoroughly wash my clothes.

While I didn't get rid of all the lice and fleas that had been plaguing me, I felt a whole lot better. When I thanked George, he just grunted at me and walked away. I was left in little doubt that he was completely disgusted with my deception, but I also knew I could count on him to keep my secret. My cousin James I wasn't nearly as sure about.

Not long after that, we captured a Union supply train. It was wonderful because that meant we had food—and shoes. In order to get to the Yankees and the supplies, we had to march for several days over a rugged mountain trail out of the Shenandoah Valley in the sleet. There was much complaining about the marching conditions we were facing.

Almost everyone felt the march was worth it when we arrived near Petersburg where a group of Federal troops was camped. The captured supply train had been going to Petersburg, and it looked like I was going to finally see battle, as this was where we were ordered to attack the Union troops.

The morning we went on the attack was thick with fog. "This is good fer us. We'll surprise 'em this way," was Mac's comment on seeing the murky fog we were going to have to go through to get to Petersburg.

Once again, I got nervous for nothing because when we arrived, the Union troops were gone, leaving plenty of supplies behind them. I could have cried for joy when the commissary issued the captured supplies. We had bacon, sugar, and real coffee.

We enjoyed the time at Petersburg very much, but it wasn't long before we were on the march again. We were going back to Orange County Court House and the little shantytown we had left in December.

I still hadn't seen battle, but I was an expert on long forced marches in cold and horrible conditions. Mac told me as we were battling against the sleet on one march, "Wait 'til we're marchin' our guts out in the burnin' sun, packin' our haversacks in July. We'll think of this freezin' trail and want ta be here."

We had halted to cross the Shenandoah River in shifts, as there were only two flatboats to pole us all across the icy river. This is when my least favorite cousin of all, James, sought me out.

James, Johnny had once told me, always had been jealous of me because I was a better boy than he was. Being a girl, I was never quite sure what that meant, except that I could always beat him in the games we played when we were young. When Johnny first told me about James' jealously, I was ecstatic. However, as I started growing into womanhood, I wasn't sure whether the insult was to James or to me. Now it didn't matter, as long as James kept my secret.

When I wasn't around James, I didn't actively worry that he would betray me. He was annoying because he liked to watch people squirm. I felt if I avoided him he would leave me alone since I wasn't an available target. His seeking me out on this early day in March while we were waiting to be ferried across the river didn't bode well for me. As soon as I realized he had come looking for me, I was immediately on the defensive.

James saw me and with a sneer shouted, "Sammie, have you heard about the girls with the 49th yet?"

He said it loud enough to ensure that everyone within five feet of us heard him. He came closer, but he didn't lower his voice one decibel.

It was Edwards who responded to James' question. "What are you talkin' about?"

"I just heard that a couple of girls dressed up like soldiers tried to attach themselves to the 49th," James shouted.

"I don't believe it for one minute," Edwards replied.

James, still shouting, said, "How about you, Sam? Can you believe girls would try to join the army?"

I was spared from responding because the flatboat had returned and it was time for us to load. I wasn't spared from James, Edwards, and Fletcher continuing to talk about whether there really could be girls marching in the 49th. They discussed little else during the crossing, and James discussed it loudly with several sly looks in my direction.

When we got off on the opposite bank, I was nervous. If James kept this up, everyone would start to wonder why my cousin was asking me such pointed questions. It didn't take long once we'd disembarked from the boat to find a crowd of soldiers openly staring at something in the middle of the group. I knew it must be the alleged girls in soldier clothes, and I had no desire to see them. I really didn't have any choice as the story had made the rounds (largely thanks to James), and there seemed to be a mad rush to look at who was causing the stir. James wasn't going to let me escape in any case.

He positioned himself firmly behind my shoulder and stayed there, pressing me forward in the crowd until we could clearly see the young ladies.

When I did lay eyes on them, I drew a sigh of relief. These girls had not even tried to hide the fact that they were female. They had not cut their hair. It had all been piled under their caps, and wisps of it were starting to fall down.

The clothes they wore actually fit, clinging to their clearly female shapes. They hadn't even tried to bind their chests at all, so their curves were clearly defined in their uniforms. I felt badly for them, as they were clearly uncomfortable with the attention they were receiving, but honestly what did they expect? Men were whistling and calling out, but naturally it was James' shouted comment that hurt me the most because it hit on my insecurities and was so clearly aimed at me.

"Maybe if ya'll weren't so pretty, you could have gotten away with your little charade, girls," James hollered.

Most of the men laughed and the girls blushed. I think I must have blushed, too, because my face felt hot. Finally, after that last barb, James let me fight my way out of the crowd, but not before I'd seen Rob Cody looking at me with an unreadable expression in his blue eyes.

That evening, our fire seemed to be the popular place to be, and I knew I was getting a quiet show of support. Besides Tom, Mac, Steve, Fletcher, and Edwards—the men who shared a fire with me nearly every night—my cousin Charles, Uncle Frank, George Smythe, and Rob Cody had come to share our evening. After talk in general, the topic that everyone had been expecting came up, brought up by Fletcher, of course.

Fletcher said, "What did ya'll think of those girls tryin' to join up?"

Edwards answered, "They can only be the wrong type of girls."

Quietly, but firmly, Rob Cody asked, "Why?"

Clearly surprised by the question, Edwards said, "A nice lady wouldn't think of joinin' up. Why would she?"

Cousin Charles said, "I can think of a number of reasons why a lady would join the army."

Snorting, Edwards said, "Name one."

"A strong belief in the Confederate cause," Charles answered quickly.

"Please." This time it was Fletcher who snorted and said, "Girls don' have any idee'r what the cause is about."

"That just shows how much you know," Charles responded with a reminiscent smile. "My wife is very aware of the cause and is one of the most flaming patriots I know." I was surprised that Charles knew his wife's views, since ladies never talked about politics...*ever.*

"But would she join the army?" Tom asked, intrigued.

"No," Charles admitted, "but that doesn't mean another woman might not if she felt strongly about the things we are fighting for."

George said, "Maybe they were trying to get away from a bad home situation."

Uncle Frank said, "Maybe they didn't have anyone to look after them at home."

"Maybe," Rob Cody said and paused, leaning forward to stir the fire with a stick. When he was sure he had everyone's attention, he continued, "Maybe they were following someone or looking for someone, a husband or a father, maybe a brother."

I thought he then threw a glance at me. "Whatever the reason, it would have to be a good one because joining up isn't worth it otherwise."

"Aw," Fletcher said, "nothin' happened to those two girls. General Thomas just ferried over to the other side of the river and told them to go on home."

Rob said, "That isn't what I meant. The risk in battle, the long enforced marches in the extreme heat or cold, and they didn't know how General Thomas would react.

"Whatever their reason, it would have to make the hunger and the mealy hardtack worth it, and the drills and the parades, the sleeping on the hard ground, and the knowledge that even if she weren't wounded or killed in battle she could just as easily die from dysentery or go crazy from the lice and the fleas. Any woman who joined the army would have to have a good and solid reason to do so." Rob looked me full in the face. "You have to admire a woman who tries, but more you have to admire one who could do it without anyone else the wiser."

He knows I thought.

SEVEN

~

Orange County Court House/Battle of the Wilderness
March-May 1864

We returned to our shanties at the Orange County Court House, much to everyone's chagrin. Despite all the marching and the harsh weather, the Shenandoah Valley had been good to us. We ate regularly and the food had been decent. The people in the Valley welcomed us wholeheartedly, and there was much less drilling and formal parade.

Now that we were back to our old camp, the drills and parade commenced again, along with food and supply shortages.

Mac, Tom, Steve, and I were delighted to find our little shanty had mostly endured our absence. We spent a couple of hours doing some very minor maintenance on the inside, and we were out of the weather again. The spring months brought lots of rain and even a snowstorm with enough accumulation for a final snowball fight between the regiments.

The camp was swept with a religious fervor that surprised me. Suddenly my hard gambling, constantly swearing comrades were being baptized and attending prayer meetings.

Rob Cody explained to me, "They are realizing the fighting will start in earnest again soon.

"This has happened before, but over the last few months there seems to be a feeling of desperation among the men that wasn't there before. I think everyone is discouraged by the way the war is going. Our government has to do so much to get recruits, but the Yanks seem to just keep coming and coming."

Comments heard around fires seemed to confirm Rob's opinion. While nobody actually said he wanted out of the army and we were fighting for a lost cause, that feeling was always under the surface of every conversation.

During those weeks we spent at Orange County Court House, I spent more time with Rob. We talked about our families and our hopes and dreams. I tried to be very careful not to let my secret slip, but sometimes I would say things that I later feared had given it away.

I was positive the night after the discussion at our campfire about the two girls in the 49th, that Rob knew I was a female. But the next day when I saw him, he treated me like he always had and I was no longer sure. I wanted badly to know if he knew the truth, but I was terrified to bring it up with him. I didn't think he would rush to the nearest officer and turn me in, but I didn't want to lose the friendship I had with him, either.

One time I attempted to discover what he'd really thought about those girls. He said, "I think they were pretty brave to try it or else really stupid."

I was hurt until he went on, "If they didn't want to be found out, they should have tried harder to look like men."

"James says only an ugly girl could pass for a soldier because any good-looking girl would be noticed in a camp full of men right away," I said.

Oh, how that assessment had hurt. While never thinking much about how I looked, I had always felt that if I wasn't a beauty I was at least a presentable young lady. James made me feel homely as a two-headed pig.

"Your cousin James is a fool. I've always thought so, ever since Johnny introduced me to him." That ended the conversation. While I still didn't know how Rob felt about girls acting like men to join the army, his disagreeing with James' opinions soothed my feelings and my ego.

Up to this point, my experience in the army had included a lot of marches and down time in camp. I had come close to fighting, but I had never had to face battle myself. While I knew I had been lucky to stay out of an actual battle for the whole time I'd been in the army (or maybe I was just fortunate that I joined at the end of the campaigning season), I knew sooner or later I'd have to face the Yankees in combat. In the beginning of May we were told to cook two days' rations, and we started to march again.

At first I thought the march would be just that, as it had been in the Valley over the winter, always marching and barely missing the Yankees or the battle. This time it wasn't to be. After we marched a couple of days, past the place all the men were guessing the Yankees were, we heard the sounds of battle. Quickly, we were ordered back to a place we'd already widely skirted.

When I encountered my first battle, I was frozen with fear. The smell of the gunsmoke was enough to make me choke with the taste of it. The battle was taking place in a wooded area. So, even if the smoke from the guns wasn't making visibility horrible, we wouldn't have been able to see anything more than a few feet in front of us.

Bodies of soldiers littered the ground and the moans of the wounded mixed with the yells of my fellow Confederate brothers in arms. My head ached and the metallic smell of blood was added to the sulfuric taste of smoke from the muskets. Beside me, Tom whooped out a loud rebel yell, and I realized our bugler was playing the "fire at will" command. In the time my head had been taking in the scene, my feet had been following my company into position.

Hearing Tom's yell snapped the horrific fascination that held me mesmerized and suddenly I heard another rebel yell. I realized the sound was being ripped from my throat and I was going through the motions that we drilled all the time in loading, priming, aiming, and firing my musket.

Throughout the afternoon, I fired and shifted my position as commanded. My throat became sore from yelling and swallowing great amounts of smoke and my eyes felt gritty. My head was pounding dully, but I was so focused on the task at hand that I hardly realized it was aching.

As dusk finally fell and we were ordered to cease firing, I realized that I was no longer in the same place where I had started. My position had changed drastically as we gained and then lost ground throughout the day. During the fighting of the day, the regiments had gotten mixed with one another. We were no longer in the companies we drilled with, the companies we fought with. When I looked around, there were a few men from my unit, but I also found I was near Rob Cody.

The first order of business was digging in—creating a protective trench. These trenches were called breastworks or works because the mounds of dirt created by digging the trenches were placed between us and the enemy, creating a hill that was about as high as our breastbone. We would fire over the hill, but the dirt would protect us as we put our heads down to reload.

Before getting whatever rest we could that night, Rob dropped down beside me with a sigh.

"Well, Sammie, you did real well in your first battle."

Grinning at him I said, "Thanks, but it is a blur in my mind. I'm not even sure what I did out there."

"Well then, you have natural instincts," Rob said.

"I'm not sure if that is good or bad," I replied. "At least natural instincts to save my own skin or follow someone else's orders to save it."

"Here," Rob grunted while handing me his canteen. "It is warmer than I like, but I bet you could use some."

Nodding eagerly, I took several deep gulps of the warm water from his canteen. I had drunk the last water from my canteen much earlier in the day.

After satisfying my thirst, I asked, "Do you think we'll have to move again?"

"Naw, we're here until dawn. I don't like the look of the crick in our line up yonder." Rob indicated a place in our line that bowed sharply toward the enemy position.

He continued, "But bringing these men into line will be the only movement tonight. Why don't you catch some sleep? I'll let you know if you need to wake for anything."

I suddenly realized that I was completely exhausted and that I'd like nothing more than to roll up in a ball on the ground and sleep for several hours.

"What about you? Aren't you tired?"

"I've dealt with the rush and the exhaustion of battle. Just sleep, I'll be fine."

I curled up with my knapsack under my head and fell quickly into a deep and dreamless sleep. The next thing I knew Rob was shaking me awake. I could tell from the dim light in the sky that it was nearly dawn. I rolled over, stretched, and then peered over the breastworks to see what was going on.

"They coming?"

"Not yet," Rob answered. "But it is nearly dawn, and with how hot the fighting was yesterday it shouldn't be long now. Get ready."

I pulled my musket out from under me and loaded it, just as men up and down the line were doing silently. Suddenly, the quiet of the morning was ripped apart as bullets came flying from every direction. They weren't just in front of us, but beside and seemingly behind us as well.

"Fire at will," called the commanders and the buglers took up the cry. I began firing at will with great concentration. With the morning mist hugging the ground and the smoke filling the air, it was difficult to tell where to shoot.

As I was reloading, the dense figures in the fog started to take the shapes of men running toward us.

"Retreat," came the command.

Rob's hand gripped my wrist and he yelled, "Come on, Sammie, retreat." I had just torn the top off my last paper cartridge with my teeth and my musket was placed with its butt on the ground, leaning against my body. When Rob grabbed my wrist, he yanked me with such force that I stumbled to my feet and followed. My musket dropped to the ground behind me.

I had barely enough presence of mind to spit out the top of the cartridge paper as Rob dragged me in a stumbling run through the dense underbrush of the woods.

I could hear the Yanks running behind trying to catch us. Every few steps I could hear one of my own comrades spit out an expletive as he looked back to see the Yanks gaining on us. I never looked back, as it took all my focus to keep up with Rob. His long legs were eating up the ground at an amazing pace, and as he continued to haul me behind him I felt like I was nearly flying. My knapsack bumped against my hip, and I felt like I couldn't get a breath.

Finally, panting, I hollered, "Rob…let…go…I…can't… keep…up."

Over his shoulder, Rob snapped, "The hell you can't." He jerked on my wrist and kept running. Just when I thought I couldn't fly one more step, we burst out of the woods onto the road and saw the most beautiful brigade of troops all dressed in dirty and shredded butternut uniforms. They were marching up the road in double quick time. I would have cheered if I could have gotten a breath to do so. Rob and I moved off to the side of the road so the division could pass us and fight the Yankees we'd just been fleeing from.

Bent over double with our hands on our knees, Rob and I stood there gulping in huge breaths of air until our heart rates slowed. After the men who had been running with us caught their breath, they let out a yell and followed our reinforcements back into the battle.

"Should we join them?" I turned to Rob with a smile of relief on my face that quickly faded when I saw his look of rage arrowed at me.

"The next time the order to retreat is given, don't you wait for one second Samantha Anne," he said in a low voice so no one else would hear.

"You know?" I said dumbly.

"Of course, I know. I've known from the start. I've just been waiting for you to confide in me," he replied tersely.

"I've wanted to, but I was afraid you would be disgusted with me."

"No," he said reaching out and brushing some of my short hair behind my ear. "Not disgusted. But don't you ever scare me like that again."

I looked at the ground in embarrassment and nodded. Forcing me to look at his face by taking my chin in his hand and pushing it up, he said gravely, "I mean it. It tore me up when I realized Johnny was gone after the battle in Gettysburg. I think it would kill me if something were to happen to you."

I blushed and kept my eyes on his as I nodded. When he was convinced I meant it, he smiled down at me and said, "Okay, Sammie Annie, let's go help these guys get the Yanks."

"I don't think I can." At his questioning look I said, "I think I dropped my musket when we started the retreat." We both started to laugh in sheer relief. Moments ago we were running for our lives, and now our biggest concern was my lack of a musket. There were no more secrets between us, and the reinforcements had the enemy on the run. So much could change in a matter of minutes. I then realized that my left hand was still clenched in a fist. I opened that hand and we started laughing even harder as we looked down at the mangled cartridge and the black powder that was all over my palm. It wasn't funny, not really, but the adrenaline coursing through us needed some release.

When we finally caught our breath and were able to stop laughing, Rob said, "Come on, we'll find you another musket." With that we headed back into the thicket of trees to fight some more with our reinforcements.

EIGHT

~

Battle of Spotsylvania
May 1864

The 14th Georgia Regiment, along with the entire battalion, went racing down the dirt road as fast as our legs would carry us. From the sounds of the battle ahead of us, our help would be needed quickly. My lungs were burning again, but I much preferred them to be burning because I was running to help Confederate soldiers rather than burning because I was running from Yankee soldiers.

The chaos of battle came into view and I could see that we'd arrived back just in time. "Back" because we were returning to where we had retreated from before dawn. We had been moved to reinforce another line when our commanding officers determined the Yankee movement in that location was decoy movement to distract us and draw our troops away from where the majority of Yankee soldiers were. We were marched back double time to where we began, arriving just in time to help the units we'd left there.

Our troops started yelling at the top of their lungs, belting out the rebel yell to alert both the Northern and Southern soldiers of our arrival. The Yankees, upon seeing and hearing us coming quickly and in great numbers, took off running. They already had scaled the works we had thrown up; now we were sending them back to their own trenches.

Shortly, we were climbing over our works after the Yanks and racing down the steep slope that separated our battle lines from those of the boys in blue. It was a heady feeling to see all those dressed in blue running away from us. I had not previously experienced a Yankee retreat since it was my second battle.

After the battle in the forest, where General Longstreet's additional troops had arrived at just the right time, we continued to fight with the Yankees for a couple of days before they slipped around us during the night. Seeing them flee now made me feel that we were finally making a difference.

The excitement of having the upper hand disappeared quickly when the Yanks tripped back into their own trenches, turned and opened fire on us. Men were falling all around me. With the rest of the men in our colors, I dropped to the ground in order to give the enemy less of a target. The bullets continued to rain around and over us.

Next to me, I could hear some desperate moaning and I turned to see Fletcher clutching his thigh with his face twisted in agony. I crawled on my belly over to him. "Let me help you."

"My leg! I think it was shot clean through the bone," Fletcher panted.

"Let me see." I scooted into a position where I could see his leg better. What I saw made me ill. There was a large hole bleeding profusely right in the middle of Fletcher's right thigh.

I knew very little about doctoring. I had learned the day that Mac and I had helped move casualties for the surgeons that a wound like this probably would result in an amputation. Of course, that was if Fletcher got back to the surgeon in time to have his leg amputated.

I just had to make sure Fletcher didn't bleed out first, lying in this field 100 yards in front of the Yankee works while bullets continued to pelt down all around us. I knew some of those bullets were finding their marks from the gasps and moans that were coming from around us.

"Got a belt?" I asked, in the most matter-of-fact voice I could manage.

Fletcher's face quickly paled and he asked, "That bad?"

"You're going to be fine, Fletcher." I repeated, "Got a belt?"

"Yeah." He paused, shifted, and grimaced, "Wife sent it...Don't think...I can...get it off."

"Okay, you just hang tight. I'll do what I can." I worked as fast as I could to pull his belt from the loops of his pants. I wrapped it tightly above his wound to stop the bleeding. As I worked, I grimly wondered if Fletcher's wife's gift of a belt would save her husband's life. Or if, no matter how hard I tried, my meager attempt at first aid would be enough until the wounded were gathered.

Numbly, I dressed Fletcher's wound to the best of my ability. Then I helped him drink from his canteen. The bullets continued to buzz constantly around us, and we kept our heads down. Finally, after what seemed like days, the order to retreat was given.

"I'm not sure if I can get you up that hill," I said to Fletcher.

Fletcher gave me a weak smile and answered, "Yer half my size, my leg is all but blowed off, ya'll be a sittin' duck. Get outta here!"

I gave him an uncertain look, and he said more forcefully, "Get outta here, kid, or ya'll be the only target climbin' up that hill."

He pushed me toward the marsh that was between me and the hill and I took off running.

I slogged through the marsh much faster than I had when I was on my way to the Yankee works. Racing up the hill, I finally reached the top and scrambled over into our trenches. My breathing was short and rapid.

"Fire at will!" came the order, and I started to speedily load my gun. Before I could shoot, Tom grabbed my arm and shouted over the noise, "Keep your head down." I nodded and saw the man to Tom's right fall back with blood trickling down the side of his head. Clearly, Tom meant what he said.

The hours until dusk seemed to fly by. From both sets of trenches, there came a gradual cease in the exchange of bullets. The light of day was giving way to early evening. Considering how the minutes dragged when we were in front of the Yankee works, I was relieved when the sun sank and we were ordered away from the lines as we needed to rest.

Our line straggled into a makeshift camp, and we started to pitch tents. We were given some food which, even if it was full of maggots, was at least something to feed our empty stomachs.

After I ate and put up a tent with Tom, I thought I needed to find Rob Cody and make sure he came through the battle all right. I was very worried about him and at the same time I felt a little foolish. I knew Rob always would see me as Johnny's little sister. I also knew I wouldn't sleep well until I could see he had come through the battle.

Before I had walked more than twenty yards, I ran into a slightly frantic-eyed Rob Cody. When he saw me, he grabbed me by the shoulders and asked in a voice that seemed somewhat panicked, "Are you okay?"

Then, he started running his hands and eyes up and down my arms. He even dropped to his knee in front of me and started running his hands down my legs, checking for any injuries.

Quickly I stepped back; I felt the heat of a blush on my cheeks. I said a little abruptly to cover my embarrassment, "I'm fine." I bent down and grabbed Rob's hands and pulled him to his feet. "I'm fine." I assured him again as I looked into his face so he would know I was being totally honest. I gazed up into his filthy face and asked, "What about you? Are you okay?"

Rob grabbed my arm and pulled me along beside him. "Come on, Sam, we're taking a walk."

I fell into step with him, and I could see he was upset as we walked away from the campfires around us. In confusion I asked, "Rob, what's wrong?" He stopped and looked around to make sure no one was within hearing distance.

"Sammie, the gig is up. It's time to admit to General Thomas that you're a female and go home."

"What?" I yelped out in shock.

Rob ran a hand through his hair and then said earnestly, "Sam, you have to go home. It's too dangerous for you to stay here."

"Rob, what are you talking about?"

Frustrated Rob answered, "You were out there today. Anything could have happened to you today. You can't stay here and get hurt or killed."

"I can't go home, Rob, you know that."

"You have to. If you don't go now and turn yourself in, I'll do it myself."

"I beg your pardon!"

Rob answered, "You heard me. You have to go home and if you don't see to it, I'll take care of it for you."

I could feel the spark of anger building inside me. "You didn't seem so upset last week when we were in battle. Why are you angry now?"

"Sammie, it's too dangerous. Last week I was with you in battle and I could take care of you. Today the whole time we were on that field, I was in agony thinking that you might be hurt. Then when we went back up the hill to our works, we were target practice for those Yanks. I knew that if you hadn't been hurt on the way down, you were surely hurt on the way back up."

"So you're saying it was fine last week because you were babysitting me?"

"Yes, I mean no. I just..."

I interrupted before he could explain. "I don't need you to watch over me. I may be a *girl* and I may have been in only two battles and I may not be as strong as the rest of you, but I can fight in this war just as well as any of you."

"Sam..."

"Fletcher got his leg blown off today. I didn't notice his greater strength or experience helped *him* any."

"Sam..."

"It could have been the same for you. I was worried about you, too, but I'm not talking about trying to get you to go home."

"Sam..."

"Besides, if you turn me in you have no idea that I'd be sent home. I could be sent to prison."

"Sam..."

I was so furious that I continued to talk over him.

"And don't try to tell me General Thomas would make sure I got home just because those girls we found coming out of the Shenandoah Valley were put on the other side of the river to find their way home. They hadn't actually been in the army. General Thomas might send me to prison just because I duped everybody for so long. I think I'm safer here facing the bullets of the Yanks than I am trying to get from here to Georgia all by myself."

Finally, Rob gripped my shoulders and gave me a little shake. "Sam, listen to me."

The shake surprised me, as did his tight grip on my shoulders. I stood looking at him with my mouth hanging open.

"Sam, I didn't mean that I was babysitting. I just meant that while you were fighting beside me I knew that you were okay. It made me a little crazy today when those bullets were coming in and I didn't know how you were."

"You being there wouldn't have made a bit of difference if I'd have been hit," I said.

"I know, but I told you once that it'd make me crazy if I lost you." Rob sounded a little desperate.

"I'm not Johnny. I'm not asking you to lose him twice."

Looking at me completely baffled, Rob answered, "I know you're not Johnny. What does Johnny have to do with it?"

"You told me it would make you crazy if you lost me, *too*. Right after that you told me how upset it made you to lose Johnny."

"Naturally, I was upset when I couldn't find Johnny. He was my best friend," Rob answered, still confused.

"He *is* your best friend. He is somewhere out there. I just have to find him."

"In-between battles?" Rob asked with a raised brow.

"Yes," I answered stubbornly.

"If you don't get hurt?"

"Robert."

"Samantha Anne," Rob mimicked.

Then he shook his head and said, "I won't be distracted. Johnny is my best friend, so, of course, I was upset in Gettysburg when I couldn't find him."

He reddened a little and then with a deep breath he said, "You are more to me than Johnny."

"Really?" I asked, in amazement.

"Really. That is why I want you to go home, where you'll be safe."

"I can't do that."

He gave me another little shake and said, "Why not?"

"I told you why not. But besides all that, there is another bigger reason."

I took a deep breath and said, "You mean tons to me, too. You have no idea what it is like at home. It is miserable, hearing reports of battles and reading about them in papers and wondering—always wondering. Waiting to hear if the people you love were involved in the fighting. Waiting for the lists to see if the people you care about have been wounded or killed or are missing, maybe taken as a prisoner by the Yankees. How can I live through that again with you? If something were to happen, no one in your family would even let me know because they don't know me."

"They know you. I've written to them all about you."

"No, Rob. I have to stay here—with you."

He looked around again, making sure that we weren't being watched. "Okay, stay here with me. But you had better take good care of yourself, you hear?"

I nodded and he pulled me into a hug. He made another quick glance around to make sure we were really alone, and then he leaned down and kissed me. When he pulled away, I'm sure my adoration for him was written all over my face because he released me abruptly. Was he thinking maybe he shouldn't touch me like I was his sweetheart?

"Come on, let's get you to your bedroll so you can be ready for tomorrow," he said gruffly. Stuffing his hands in his pockets, he lead back toward my campsite.

NINE

~

Battle of Jericho Mills
May 1864

I leaped over the edge of the embankment. Just as I started sliding down the deep edge of the ravine I felt a stinging burn in my upper right shoulder. Then I heard the blast of the shell. I slipped and slid down the bank while dirt clods and debris flew everywhere.

Soldiers were scrambling down the embankment all around me. My feet hit the railroad bed at the bottom of the gorge, and I allowed myself to slide to a sitting position. Another shell exploded above us and the dirt rained down again. Leaning my head against the dirt behind me, I closed my eyes and listened to the chaos around me.

I was so tired. We were in this grueling battle with the Yankees forever, it seemed. Every day, in rain and in sun, we fought on and on. Just as we thought we were making up ground, the Yanks would be gone the next morning—slipping off and around us and closer to Richmond. So we followed, slogging though rivers and plodding along roads covered in dust or mud.

We stopped for short rests and skirmishes with retreating Federals as we overtook the ends of their columns of marching soldiers. Sometimes we took prisoners and sometimes we just traded volleys of shot. Today had looked like a promising victory—a solid gain over the enemy, and then everything fell apart before my eyes.

We were pushing the Yankees back, having surprised them as we came out on their right from some underbrush. We'd battled our way through their lines before they even knew we were there. They retreated and we came forward quickly, taking the land the enemy once held. And then suddenly, out of nowhere, came Union reinforcements. Artillery guns started shredding huge holes in our front. Before I knew where we were, our fighting formation had broken and everyone started running to the rear.

Dirt rained down on us as shells exploded near the top of the ravine where I had taken cover. I could hear other soldiers scrambling down the embankment. I reached down and pulled off my shoe and emptied it of dirt. In the last three days, we'd marched somewhere around thirty miles. My boots, which were full of holes before this campaign started, were little more than strips of leather held together with string. Sliding down the embankment with my feet first wasn't too good on my shoes.

"How long before you throw them out altogether?" asked Tom had slid onto the railway bed beside me.

"Who knows? The last thing I want is to have to run over ground like that with nothing at all," I answered.

"You'd better scavenge some soon, or that's exactly what you'll be doing," Tom advised.

I wrinkled my nose in distaste at my shoes and knowing he was right. I was more upset that now the thought of taking boots off a fallen man didn't disgust me nearly as much as it had when Tom first mentioned it to me a month ago.

I suppose that meant I was becoming a hardened veteran. I didn't know whether that should make me want to cry out in despair or swagger with pride. I finished lacing up what was left of my boot and leaned my head back against the ravine wall.

☙

I must have drifted off to the sound of musket fire above me and the smell of dirt and blood around me. Voices raised in extreme anger jerked me awake. Rubbing my eyes, I sat up and peered around. The line of men was silent as they leaned against the embankment that stretched out on both sides of us.

The light in the ravine was hazy, and General Thomas was listening as General Wilcox berated us for our conduct. I was too far away to hear exactly what was being said, but the tone of General Wilcox's voice was clearly that of a superior officer scolding someone under him. The attitude of the men who were close enough to hear the words of General Wilcox seemed to shift from being uncomfortable to being angry.

None too soon for the men, General Wilcox galloped off on his stallion. At the same time, we received orders to fall in. The march took us to Anderson's Station where we would rest for the night while the officers tried to determine where the Yankee leader, General Grant, had positioned his men.

As we settled in for the night, news of General Thomas being told off by General Wilcox was the topic of conversation around every campfire. We were being blamed for turning tail and finding safety in the railroad gorge.

"I'd like to see how cool that windbag Wilcox is in front of the guns," Tom said with disgust after the information reached our fire.

"It weren't us that broke in the first place," Mac replied. "I wanna know why we git the blame when everyone knows it's those Joes from South Carolina that started the run."

"That's right," added Steve Jones. "If they'd been where they should have been, there'd have been no trouble taking that ridge."

"Truth is, we'd all be in much better shape if Wilcox would stay still for two days together," Tom replied. "That way the wagons would catch up and we'd finally have something to eat."

"Ain't even anythin' around to scavenge," Mac said in agreement.

"Wouldn't matter much anyway," I said, "All they're going to bring us is hardtack full of weevils."

Tom and Mac laughed. Mac said, "Ya been in this army too long. What happened ta all those green dreams ya brought here with ya?"

Tom said, "It is a shame to see a fellow so gloomy about life before he even starts to shave."

Mac said laughing, "Ain't that the truth. When ya goin' ta get hair on yer face like a real man?"

I retorted, "I'd rather not, thanks. I've got enough lice crawling all over me without tempting them with a beard."

"Yer all right, kid," said Mac and gave me a friendly thump on my shoulder.

I gasped in a sob as pain shot through me. Mac said worriedly, "Kid, what's wrong? Ya just went white as death."

I turned toward the fire and tried to get a good look at my shoulder. Tom said sharply, "What's that all over your sleeve?"

"Blood," Mac answered. "When'd ya get nailed, kid?"

"I don't know," I replied. "But it can't be that bad. I only just felt it."

"It doesn't matter," Tom said firmly. "It's off to the surgeon's tent you go."

"No."

"They'll be busy for a while yet with the bad cases, but you can't fight with a bullet in your arm."

"No."

"Don't give me any more lip and stop being a baby about it. They'll stitch you up and have you back in the front lines by tomorrow."

"No." I nearly yelled it this time.

I couldn't go to the surgeon's tent with any kind of wound but mostly not with a wound where they'd cut off my tunic. My deception would be revealed if the surgeons discovered I was a girl.

"I'm going to my cousin." I stated firmly, as if I was sure that was the best thing to do.

Mac said, "C'mon kid, it ain't that bad. Doc'll stitch ya up an' everythin' will be fine."

"I'm going to my cousin," I said again. "He'll stitch me up just fine, and then I'll be back without anyone else the wiser."

Tom said, "Son, if your cousin can stitch at all, he'd have been grabbed by the sawbones long before now. Let's go get you taken care of right."

"He can stitch if he needs to. He just doesn't like to. He'll stitch me."

With that parting shot, I got up and went in search of Charles. Tom tapped out his pipe and followed me. He didn't say anything more about going to a real doctor, which I was grateful for. We wandered for some time before we finally came to Uncle Frank's fire.

I was not surprised to find these men also grumbling about how General Thomas had been treated at the hands of General Wilcox earlier that day. Also not surprising was that the complaints were very much the same as what was said at our fire.

When they noticed Tom and me in the dim light of the fire, my cousin James said with a sneer, "Well lookie here, if it ain't my ugly cousin, Sammie, and his friend. You going to join us in a little insubordination and grump about being blamed for running—I mean retreating—when things got too hot this afternoon?"

Charles said, "Quiet down, James. Tom, Sam, how're things over in your area of our happy little camp?"

I looked first at Charles and said, "I've got a little problem and I need your help."

Surprised, Charles answered, "Okay, cousin. Let's hear it."

I looked at James who was scowling at us; then I looked back at Charles and said, "Do you think I could talk to you alone for a minute?"

James sneered at me. "Out with it, Sammie, you're in the bosom of your family and friends."

Uncle Frank spoke sharply to James who then stormed away in a huff. "Don't listen, Sammie. He's irritated by the way things turned out this afternoon."

Charles added, "James never likes to be seen as anything but a conquering hero. The fact that he ran as fast as any of us doesn't sit too well with him."

George Smythe added quietly with a smile, "Faster than any of us, you mean."

When Charles laughed, Uncle Frank said sternly, "Okay, boys, we were all headed for cover. No one is judging here tonight."

Tom cleared his throat and said, "Sam's bleeding, probably all day, and won't go up to the surgeon's tent."

The three men stared at Tom after hearing his blunt statement. I shot him a glare and then said, "Charles, you know I can't go to the surgeon. Besides, I know it can't be that bad. I didn't even feel it until just a minute ago."

"Come on, Sam, I'll look at it," Charles said seriously. I followed him toward his knapsack, which he had tossed three feet away from the fire. I heard George Smythe as he got up and left in a huff after James. Tom settled down by the dying fire with Uncle Frank, who took it upon himself to distract Tom from anything going on my way.

Charles took the bayonet off the muzzle of his musket and stuck it point down in the ground. Rummaging around in his knapsack, he found a candle stub that he stuck in his makeshift candleholder—the bayonet. "Lucky for you I had furlough not so long ago. I have some things here that I normally wouldn't have. Let me see it."

I turned my shoulder toward the light from the candle Charles had just lit.

Charles sighed. "Sammie, honey," he said quietly. "I can't see what is wrong with your tunic on. That's why you are avoiding the doc, right."

Blushing hotly, I nodded. Then I turned away and unbuttoned my shirt. When I slipped my arm out of my tunic, I felt a tug at my skin, followed by a sting as the sleeve tore free from my wound. I draped the left side of my shirt over my chest as best as I could and was grateful I was facing away from the fire. With the dancing shadows of the candle and the swath of cotton binding my chest, I was still fully covered. Even so, I couldn't help feeling completely exposed—the rigid modesty of my childhood being totally ingrained in me.

Charles distracted me with idle chatter while he washed the wound with fresh water from his canteen. He was telling me how he'd found things at home during his furlough six weeks earlier when a new figure appeared before the fire. Up until then, I was watching Charles wipe the blood off my arm.

"Where's Sammie?" Rob asked in a voice that cracked like a whip.

"Rob boy, good to see you," Uncle Frank answered as he glanced at Tom.

Rob completely ignored Uncle Frank and said, "I'm here to see Sammie."

He then saw Charles and me, walked around the fire, and crouched down so his face was at my level.

"What happened? George came to me and mumbled something about you getting hurt."

Charles answered, "It isn't a big deal, Rob. Just a scratch. It looks like she got stung by something that just grazed her."

"Oh, that's right," I said as I recalled when my arm first started hurting. "As I was going over the embankment today, I felt something hit me in the arm. It stung. By the time I got to the bottom, my boots were so full of rocks and I was just so tired and hungry that the burning in my arm didn't seem to matter."

"It didn't," Charles agreed, "but next time it might matter a little more, so pay attention, okay?"

I nodded in agreement. Charles said, "Sam, I'm going to clean this out real good and stitch it up as the cut is deeper than I like. You have to keep it clean though so you won't get an infection, you hear?"

After I nodded, he said again, "Lucky for you I still have what I need, otherwise those medics would have you kicked out of this army so fast your head would swim."

Rob said sarcastically, "Yeah, lucky. We wouldn't want her sent home or anything where she might be safe."

Charles responded, "She's better off here, where we can watch her. Who knows what other kind of schemes she may concoct to try to find Johnny."

"Not that this one has gotten me very far," I said with a stab at lightness. I wanted to try and convince Rob that his wanting me to leave hadn't hurt nearly as much as it actually had.

Rob sighed. "It scares me to death to have you in front of those guns day and night."

"Don't worry," I told him trying to smile. "The bullets that were meant for me missed me today." I sucked in a breath as pain stabbed through my arm. Rob took my hand and squeezed it as Charles got ready to make a second stitch.

"Just ignore whatever Charles is doing."

"I don't think I can. It hurts," I replied.

"Have I ever told you about how Johnny and I met?" Rob asked. I shook my head. Rob started spinning tales to keep my mind off my arm, and Charles took his time to make sure the wound was clean, stitched, and protected.

TEN

Petersburg, Virginia
December 1864-January 1865

The days became weeks, the weeks became months, and we continued our game of tag with the Yankees. They dug in and we dug in—close enough in some cases to have conversations with each other over the works. Musket fire was fairly consistent up and down the lines as small skirmishes would erupt and just as suddenly end.

After a time—sometimes a day, sometimes a week, sometimes longer than that—the Yankees would shift their position and go around us. We'd march double time to catch up with them and cut them off. With every movement the Yankees got a little closer to Richmond. Through torrential rains and scorching heat, both armies continued the standoff.

Then we hit a true halt near Petersburg, Virginia. There we stayed, fighting skirmishes and shouting over the lines until winter overtook us again. It was necessary to call a halt for two days to make winter quarters on both sides of the lines. Instead of building huts, we dug holes that were then covered with logs and branches.

I was not thrilled with our new quarters, but Tom scoffed at me and told me I'd find them "very comfy." Our hut looked too much like a grave to me, being dug six-feet deep—but wide enough for four of us—for me to be excited about sleeping there. To my surprise the hole was warm, and it also protected us from Yankee shells and the minnie balls spit out of Yankee muskets.

The one thing that became increasingly clear through that long year of chasing and standoff was that the Yankees were wearing us down.

Dysentery struck us hard and repeatedly. The gut-wrenching diarrhea hit so quickly, a person had very little time to find a place to be ill. Dysentery weakened the body and sometimes even caused death. Everyone in the Confederate army fought it at least once over those months of chasing down the blue coats.

I was lucky in that every time dysentery made the rounds again, I had "light" cases of the illness. My cases were light enough that I didn't have to go to the surgeons, who couldn't do anything for the sickness anyway. Still, I was convinced the cramps in my belly would kill me if they got any worse.

It was an added challenge while I was disgustingly sick to find decent cover so no one would find out I was a girl. But this probably kept me from getting sicker as I couldn't use the latrine pits with the rest of the sick men. My isolation probably saved me from the severe clutches of the illness that was plowing through our numbers.

The skirmishes over the works were taking their toll. Generally, the men hit didn't die, but often their injuries were severe enough to send them to a bigger hospital in Richmond.

Charles was one of those casualties. While I worried about him, I couldn't help thinking that it was good he'd gotten away from the front line. His wound was bad enough that as soon as he regained his strength, he would probably be sent home to his young wife and daughter.

Hunger was another major issue we were facing. While I couldn't imagine the Yankees escaped the dysentery entirely, they clearly escaped the hunger. We were close enough to smell their cookfires at different times of the day. Oh, how the smell of anything at all would tempt us. We had to make due with hardtack that was hard enough to break teeth and also full of bugs. As we continued to lose weight, the Yankees were filled out to the point of looking fat to our eyes.

Our glimpses of the enemy told us other things as well. Our clothes were tattered, while they had decent clothes and shoes. For a while, I envied those men whose shoes weren't just a strip of leather like mine. Then one day Tom tossed a pair of boots at me. They were scuffed some, but there still was a lot of wear in them. Best of all, these boots were only slightly big on me. Tom saw the look of surprise on my face. Before I could say anything, he held up his hand to stop my words.

"You don't want to know. Just cover your feet and don't ask questions."

I realized that I really didn't want to know more. I knew the boots had come off a dead soldier. He probably was young since most of my comrades had feet considerably larger than mine—even those close to my age.

I nodded my thanks to Tom and pulled the boots on my feet, trying not to think about the previous owner. It bothered me more than a little that once I had the boots on, I could put out of my mind where they came from. I wondered if that meant I was getting hardened by war.

Two nights later Tom had some sardines he shared around. They tasted fantastic, especially since our food rations were so scarce. I wondered where he got the food, so I asked him.

"Maybe I'll tell you tonight," he said. I was not satisfied with his answer, but he grinned and sat back silently.

◊

That night, Tom woke me and whispered that I should follow him and to bring the tobacco I had in my knapsack.

We quietly made our way through camp to where the picket lines were and found nobody on duty. I gave Tom a glance and he shrugged, "They're probably playing poker with the Yankees."

I was surprised, but then Tom shocked me even more by going out into the land between our camp and the Yankee camp and giving a shrill whistle. Another whistle answered and we made our way to a small campfire set between the two army lines.

"Who is the boy?" a Yankee soldier asked Tom.

"Sam, meet Ben, Jasper and Alan. Boys, this is Sam."

The three men grunted a response, and Tom and I sat down at the fire with them. Tom talked to two of the men like they were old friends. Ben didn't have very much of an accent and was easy to understand. Jasper was near impossible to understand because of his thick Northern accent. The third sat as silent and watchful as I was. While they talked over all kinds of subjects, no one said a word about the war.

As I studied the men and listened to them talk with Tom, I realized the third man in their group seemed different than the other two. His hair was starting to get long, and the light playing on his face from the fire made his features look delicate. He looked almost like a woman when the fire flared just right. It suddenly struck me that there might be girls who had run off to join the Union army as I had done. I thought about the wounded woman I had treated. What was her story? What was "Alan's" story?

Alan caught me staring at him (or was it her) and glared. I focused again on Tom and noticed the two men he was talking to looked a lot like him. They talked for over an hour, then Tom said, "Sam's got some tobacco to trade."

"There's nothing like home-grown tobacco," said Ben. "We have sugar and soap to trade. We noticed you could do with some soap the last time we met," Ben added laughing.

Tom gave him a jab on his shoulder and laughed, "You're right. Sam is always complaining about the bugs."

Tom did the bartering and I gave the Yanks the tobacco I got as my ration and could never use, even to convince people of my manliness. In exchange, they gave us a bag of sugar and two bars of soap.

I noticed the third Yankee, the one I thought was a girl, filled a pipe with the tobacco right away. Despite the pipe, I was convinced he was a she.

As we went back to the camp, unchallenged by the guard, I asked Tom how he'd come to meet the Yankees. "Ben is my brother," was Tom's reply. He must have noticed my shock because he went on.

"When he was seventeen, Ben left home to go help on my Uncle's farm in Pennsylvania. Jasper is our cousin who owns the farm now. Ben bought the place that lays north of Jasper's. By the time the war started, Ben had lived in the North for as long as he'd lived in Georgia.

"Did you barter for my boots from Ben?"

"Yes, they have a lot more supplies than we do. But they can't get the good Southern tobacco like we can."

After that first evening, I went with Tom to see Ben and Jasper often. We talked of many things on those nights, but never the war. Sometimes Alan was there—more often he wasn't. The more I saw of him, the more I was convinced that he was just like me.

Even with the distraction of the enjoyable evenings at the Yankee campfires, it was hard to miss the difficulties our army was facing.

Our casualties were climbing, while at the same time the enemy never seemed to have a hole in their lines. One morning at reveille we awoke to find a whole company gone. Reports were later confirmed that those men had simply thrown down their weapons and crossed the trenches with a white shirt flapping. Rob and Mac were completely disgusted.

"Now those blue coats will know everythin'," Mac said in disgust.

"It was bad enough to be losing one or two at a time—even those who are deserting to go home—but a whole company." Rob shook his head.

I understood his frustration, but Rob's irritation surprised me. I knew Mac really hated the Yankees, but I hadn't thought Rob felt the same way.

The next time I found him by himself, I asked Rob, "Why did you join the army?"

Rob shrugged and said, "Seemed like the honorable thing to do."

He must have seen the frustration in my face because he added, “I wasn’t very interested in states’ rights and wasn’t much into politics. At the beginning of the war, Johnny and I were the same age. Do you remember why he joined? We were both young men hoping for a chance to show how heroic we were when it came to battle. I didn’t even try to get elected as an officer because I was going to rise from the bottom of the group on my merits. By the time reality hit, I was happy to stay with the enlisted men.”

“Why?” I asked, confused and thinking he would make a good officer.

“Because that is where the true heroics are happening, even if most of them never get acknowledged.”

“Do you hate the Yankees like Mac does?”

Rob simply shook his head. “No.”

“Then why are you so upset about the deserters?”

Rob took a long time before he answered. “Look, Sammie, we’re losing this war. It’s just a matter of time. While I know we’re going down, I’d rather go down swinging, not because someone got fed up with the cold or the hunger or the lice and ran to the other camp and gave them another ace. The Yanks are already winning. We don’t need someone who fought with us giving them even more information.”

The deserters were not always heading across the lines. Many of them went home—simply tired of fighting and wanting to protect their families from the oncoming tide of Northerners. Many times, we didn’t really know where a missing man had gone. We would wake up in the morning and his bedroll would be empty. One morning I heard that my cousin James' bedroll had been found empty, and Uncle Frank was angry enough to talk about disowning him.

The morale of our army was also down because of all the moves we were making. With every march to race and block General Grant and his Yankee army, we were being pushed farther into our own territory. At the same time, the Yankees were moving farther away from their loved ones.

Also, we weren't getting any mail to reassure us of conditions at home. What we were getting was especially horrible news to everyone in my company of Georgians. Reports were that the Yankee General Sherman was marching with his armies across our state, burning everything in his way. While these reports worried us to distraction about our families and our homes, they were victories of great importance to those men in the other ditch.

One evening after hearing how close Sherman and his armies were to our home county, George Smythe came and sought me out. I was surprised, since he'd made his disgust of me very apparent a year ago, when he stood guard while I bathed in a freezing river. While he hadn't exactly avoided me since then, he'd never sought me out either. I saw him only when I went to his mess to talk with my Uncle Frank or my cousins. He seemed shy as he approached me, which was surprising since he'd always seemed so confident when we were younger and disgusted after I'd joined the army.

Clearing his throat he asked, "Did you hear about Sherman's latest burnings?"

I nodded and said, "I think he'll pass by our folks, though. He's too far south."

"He could go any way and you know it. The man's a loose cannon," George replied.

I said, "We all know he's going to Atlanta. Why would he target a sleepy little backwater like ours?"

"I wish I was there to take care of Mother and Bella," he said quietly.

I was surprised that he had confided in me, but I realized he must be looking for reassurance.

I told him, "Don't worry about your family. They will be fine."

Then I pointed to my butternut uniform covered with patches and full of lice and fleas. "We women are tougher than you think."

George relaxed and a weak smile crossed his face. We didn't say anything for a few moments, but when he finally spoke it was without anger.

"When I saw you in that uniform there at Orange County Court House, I was so furious with you I could hardly see."

"Why?"

"I guess I'd decided you were a fragile flower that I was meant to protect," George said blushing. He continued to explain, "That was stupid because you always were a tagalong tomboy who never would leave Johnny alone. I guess since I ran interference for you with James, I saw myself as your special protector. I've been thinking a lot about how you went from fragile flower to Confederate warrior.

"I finally realized that while you always accepted my interference with James, it was because he was slyly mean. Even when you gave up following Johnny around to start being the lady your momma wanted you to be, there was determination behind your delicate looks and you could have handled James on your own."

After a pause, George continued, "When you showed up here, I was only seeing the young lady I left in a big hoop skirt and picture hat. Instead, you were the little girl with ragged braids who didn't even cry after falling out of the apple tree. I just knew that I couldn't protect you from the ugliness of battle or shield you from the way men are when there are no women around. I also was sure you'd shame all of us by running the first time you saw what fighting really is."

I was ready to protest his last statement, but George silenced me with a look. "I guess I'm saying I'm sorry I haven't stood by you in the army when you probably needed me most."

"Don't worry, I've done fine. I haven't been completely on my own here at this camp. Besides, if I had it to do all over, I'd never have left home on a useless search for Johnny. I certainly wouldn't have joined the army. In some ways I wish you could have protected me from my stupidity."

Standing in silence again, I saw Rob Cody coming toward us. He arrived in time to hear George say, "I just hope momma and Bella will be as strong as you are if Sherman takes it in his head to veer north instead of heading straight to Atlanta."

"He is going to Atlanta," I answered firmly. "Besides, they will be fine. We are all stronger than you men have ever credited us."

George finally seemed relieved. Then after talking a few minutes to Rob, he left as it was time for him to go to picket duty.

Rob asked me casually, "Did he finally figure out that with most of us men at war, the women are running things in our absence and doing a fine job of it?"

I grinned and said, "Oh, he hasn't gotten that far yet. But now he knows if Sherman takes it in his head to face his mother and sister, they will be able to hold the Yanks off with more than their knitting needles and embroidery hoops."

Smiling a little wickedly, Rob asked, "Did you or did you not tell him that his sister learned to shoot from Johnny after he taught you to shoot?"

"How did you know about that?"

"Johnny told me how he caught you showing off your shooting abilities to the girl and how angry he was with you."

"Angry doesn't begin to cover it. He was absolutely furious. After giving us a tremendous scolding, he taught

Isabella himself so that I didn't do it wrong and kill someone in the process."

"He was proud of you all the same," Rob said after he stopped laughing.

Sarcastically, I replied, "That was clear by the way he shook me after Bella had gone home." Then I said, "I'm surprised he remembered it. He never spoke of it again after that day."

☙

Despite all our setbacks, General Lee's army was not defeated. As always when it looked the darkest, a little humor would pull us through. It was not uncommon to hear laughter around the campfires, even when there was nothing in the cooking pot to eat.

Another revival of sorts also started. It was strange for me to see hardened gamblers throw out their decks of cards and men who turned the air blue with their cursing start curbing their tongues just in case they didn't make it through the next skirmish. Many of the unconverted scoffed at the newly religious, but those who always had been pious welcomed them with open arms into the fold. I was happy to let everyone go their own way, especially since I really didn't want anyone examining my true motivations.

So the months passed with us in a standoff with the Northern army. We were hungry, sick, and worried. But we weren't beaten—at least not yet.

ELEVEN

Fort Gregg
March 1865

My yell lingered in the air as I ran toward the recently lost picket lines, my brothers in arms hollering and running forward beside me. A dizzying adrenaline rush pumped through me, drowning out that sick fear I had come to know before a battle. Boy, these Northerners were stubborn and not giving up any ground as the tide of gray swept toward them. Raising my musket, I stopped and fired at the Yankee blocking my own forward rush. I barely noticed the look of surprise as his weapon dropped. I already was racing past him as blood soaked his tunic, and he raised his hand to his left shoulder to stop the bleeding. Somewhere in my subconscious, I noted that he was young—probably younger than I—and his black wispy mustache and stubble of beard still had the downy look of first growth.

During the heat of battle, I was unaware of these details. These scenes came back in clearer detail when there were no bullets flying over my head.

I heard my voice in my version of what had become known as the rebel yell as I passed the boy I shot. I went down on my knee to reload as I arrived at the picket trench. All around me was the action of battle, and I was a greedy participant. I loaded and reloaded to constantly fire until the yell of victory rose over the retaken picket line.

Before the echo of that victory shout died, men in blue tumbled over the breastworks in front of us. I let go of the ball that was primed in my musket and raced back over the ground I'd just covered. With adrenaline still carrying me, I saw—but didn't think about—Steve Jones clubbing a Yankee with the butt of his musket. There was no time to reload before they were on us again. I again passed the boy I'd shot, and he was still struggling to stop the bleeding from his wound. I made it through the opening in the line of reserve troops before they closed ranks and started firing to keep the Yanks at the picket lines instead of coming farther into our territory.

I stood doubled over with my hands on my slightly bended knees, gasping for air. Tom was beside me, breathing heavily. The rush of battle slowly faded and Tom said as he panted, "I'm too old for this sort."

I think I managed a weak smile as I began looking around. Mac was there but no Steve. In nearly every battle since the beginning, the four of us had fought shoulder to shoulder. Mac and Tom flanked Steve and me, helping protect us as much as they could. "Where's Steve?"

Mac straightened up and looked back, his eyes narrowing. Finally he shrugged and said, "Guess he fell behind."

That's when I started thinking more rationally. It happened after every battle when my emotions were more settled, but never quite so suddenly as now. I realized I had gotten a really good look at the boy I'd shot. I also realized while I always hoped my bullets would hit their targets, this was the first time I really knew one of them had. Never before had I been close enough to see the actual results of my shots. Of course, I had seen the wounded and dead, but they could have been the victims of anyone's musket.

It was clear to me now when I had seen Steve using his musket as a club that he was being overtaken by the enemy. There was no escape for him and surely he would be taken to a prisoner-of-war camp somewhere in the North. My own self-preservation instincts were running so high then, I didn't understand what I had seen until it was too late.

I started shaking uncontrollably and rushed to find a place to be sick. I hadn't eaten anything of real substance for so long, when I found some bushes and hit my knees in front of them, there was nothing inside me to get rid of. So I just heaved and shook over and over and let the tears stream down my face.

I don't know how long I was curled up over my knees in front of those bushes before I heard Tom ask, "You okay, kid?" I shook my head *NO*. Then Mac, more gruffly, said, "You seen it all afore. What's wrong wi' ya?"

I couldn't tell them how wrong my decision was to come and join this army. I had long regretted joining, realizing there was really no way to find Johnny through his old unit. But I'd still hoped to discover where he was.

Now, I had witnessed Steve's capture without even knowing what I really was seeing until it was too late.

I actually saw the results of my own bullet hitting that young Federal soldier.

Yes, I knew with a certainty that it was too late for Johnny. He'd been missing for two years—lost somewhere on the soil of Pennsylvania. If Johnny hadn't flat out died on that battlefield—and no one in his unit would have realized it with all the chaos—he would have rotted away to nothing in a Yankee prison camp.

While on this hopeless crusade to find my never-to-be-found brother, I had lost a huge piece of myself. I could never forget the things I seen, never take back the minnie balls I'd shot, nor erase the hardships I'd experienced in the army. Always inside me there would be a dark place that would not have been there if I had stayed home to worry with my parents like I was expected to.

Did the others feel they'd lost the best of themselves during their time in the war? Did Mac or Tom ever question why they were here? Had Rob or Johnny? Did the Yankee soldier, Alan, ever wish she had stayed home instead of joining the army?

Mac and Tom were still waiting for an answer, so I finally said, "I realized Steve was gone, and it gave me the shakes. I'll be fine in a minute."

Mac, still sounding gruff, but with that surprising kindness he sometimes showed, said, "Gives me the shakes too. Sometimes I forget how young ya are, kid, 'cause ya carry yerself when the shootin' starts."

Tom, lightening the mood said, "How can you forget he's just a kid? He doesn't even have a shadow of a whisker yet."

I gave them a weak smile and replied how I was expected, "Least I don't have bugs eating up my face."

Mac slapped my shoulder and said, "C'mon, kid, we gotta get back. Them Yanks've sure held that picket line. Our muskets'll be needed."

Bitterly, Tom mumbled, "More than ever before."

They were both right. We were at low count when it came to men able to fight. Even our officer staff was in trouble for numbers due to illnesses and desertions we'd suffered through the winter.

As the ground started to thaw, we pulled back to do some regrouping just south of Petersburg. Regrouping hadn't gone so well, though, because the Yanks were right on our heels. They continually gained ground, while we continued to weaken and our numbers diminished daily.

For a week we went back and forth with the Yankees. The men from the North just kept coming; still we held what ground we could.

Holding that ground continued to be a challenge. General Grant moved to our right, so our lines were stretched to the right to stop him. Still we held, even though there was more and more space between each man on the line. The rain poured and still we held—until we could hold no more.

ᘓ

The nightmare of a battle started when most nightmares do, in the wee hours of the morning. The artillery regiments were exchanging fire all night. We knew an attack was coming, but we didn't know when or where it would happen. The pickets swapped some musket fire and then everything went absolutely silent. It was a penetrating silence—like nothing I'd heard or felt since I'd joined the army. Terrifying is the only way to describe the horrible silence that fell in the middle of that night. We knew an attack must be coming. But from where? When? Those questions haunted us in the eerie silence.

The darkness was still thick around us when the Yankees attacked suddenly and straight at the defenses being held by my regiment. The attack shattered the stillness as it shattered our lines of defense. Some of us retreated quickly. Those who stayed to fight paid the price of either capture or death.

I didn't need to be told twice to get out of the way of the army that was taking man after man in our regiment as prisoners. Our retreating columns were in complete disarray and growing more chaotic all the time. Every time I looked back, as dawn brought more sunlight, it seemed the number of Yankees was multiplying. For those of us in gray, the panic was raging.

There were crazy sights all around during that mad retreat. Several times I saw men throwing down their muskets and sitting on the ground in despair, waiting for the Yankees to capture them. Here and there groups of infantry would rally and turn back to fight, only to be stopped and quickly scattered again.

I saw a man from a captured artillery unit fighting the enemy with a cannon's long-handled rammer. It was the only weapon he had. I also saw several men retreating into the undergrowth rather than making their way back to Fort Gregg. The majority of our officers were at Fort Gregg trying to regroup, and a counterattack certainly would be made.

Most of us raced to the protection of Fort Gregg, where we believed someone in authority could piece together the broken units into some sort of cohesive front.

I was following on the heels of Tom and Mac, racing to Fort Gregg when an officer rode up. He shouted directions and ordered a couple of defensive lines to be set up. I found myself being sent away from the Fort and defending a stretch of land near some woods that flanked it. I thought our defensive line was thin before, but now I realized how much thinner we could be stretched.

Fort Gregg and Fort Whitworth were at capacity, and those on the defensive lines around the Forts were placed as far apart to remain only within hailing distance. With the undergrowth, I couldn't see the men on either side of me, but I could hear them over the noise of battle if they shouted or whistled loudly enough. Finally the order was given for those of us on the defensive line to fall in retreat.

The Yankees didn't seem interested in trying to flank the Forts. Both before and after our full-scale retreat, I did not see one bluecoat coming toward me. The Yankees didn't need to flank us because they had us beat in sheer numbers.

As we were ordered to retreat, we passed within sight of the Fort. All I could see was Federals scaling the walls of the Fort. I broke ranks to run to the Fort, but the man in line behind me grabbed my shoulder and pulled me back into the line. Furious, I struggled to break free from the strong grasp. I turned and swung. As my fist connected with his chin, I saw Rob Cody's eyes through the gunpowder and dirt smeared on his face. I was flooded with so many emotions I almost went completely limp. I took a deep breath and tugged away, blurting, "Tom and Mac are in there. I saw them going that way."

"They won't thank you for getting captured with them." Rob yelled.

"But..."

"They protected you for two years. They don't want you in that Fort right now."

Grudgingly, I fell back into ranks with Rob one step behind me.

ᘛ

We marched to the Appomattox River and crossed it that night. For the next week, we continued to move westward, but our steps were dogged by a victorious and jubilant Yankee contingent.

Every day, more of our men were missing, every day the supply wagons were delayed, and every day those bluecoats got closer. Finally, they caught up to us and forced the end of our retreating column to fight a bloody battle.

The day after our rearguard battled those persistent Northerners, General Lee asked for a peace agreement. We had lost the war.

TWELVE

~

Appomattox Court House
April 1865

The best thing about the week we spent at Appomattox was the food. Once the peace treaty was signed, the Union supply wagons started distributing food to the Confederate army. We got full rations and that was more food than we'd seen in months. Some of the men were bitter about eating food the Yankees provided us, but I noticed that nobody turned away their rations.

Another good thing was that our mail finally caught up with us. We had not had news from our families since before we'd been in Petersburg. I had not gotten any mail since joining the army. No one knew where I was. My relatives in the 35th had all decided not to say anything to the people at home. The fewer people who knew exactly where I was, the less likely I would be discovered.

While I didn't get any mail, other men getting news from home lightened the mood in camp. Now that the war was over, we were all looking forward to going home.

The worst thing about our week encamped at Appomattox was watching the dejection of General Lee while he was meeting and negotiating the terms of our surrender. Every time he passed through the camp, the men cheered him with tears running down their faces. General Lee was assured over and over by the men that we had been willing to continue fighting. He smiled sadly, and he said how proud he was of us and how sorry he was that he'd failed us. That, of course, brought more tears. Seeing so many men crying was upsetting to me. I had never seen a grown man cry, and these toughened veterans were the very last people I expected to be the first men I saw in tears.

These men had given up nearly everything to answer the call to follow General Lee, and the result was not a Confederate victory. This feeling of failure to our states, our families, our General, and ourselves was overwhelming in the camp. It was little wonder tears were shed. Even understanding the reason behind the tears didn't make seeing the men cry any easier for me.

Finally, the terms of surrender were completed and General Lee left the camp for the last time. The following morning we lined up in companies and regiments, officially stacked our muskets and surrendered to the Federal army.

Despite having fought us bitterly for the past four years, the men of the Union army saluted us as we performed this ritual of surrender. I stacked my musket along with the few men remaining in my unit, took my oath of loyalty to the United States of America, and went to the Union General's Aide who was writing everyone's discharge papers.

"Name?"

"Samuel Davis," I answered for probably the last time.

I didn't even look at the paper he handed me, just stuffed it in my pocket and headed back to my camp. Rob was not too far behind me, and in silence we packed our belongings. Still quiet in our thoughts, we left the camp together. Everything I was feeling was hard to put into words, and I guess it was the same for Rob. Too much relief that the war was over, too much anger that so many lives had been lost, too much guilt for being alive when so many weren't, too much sorrow for a lost cause, and mostly too much grief for the loss of the men I'd come to depend on in the regiment.

When the camp was no longer in sight, Rob broke the silence between us. "You did real well. Johnny would be proud of you."

"I don't feel like I did real well. Especially now that I'm going home. I feel like I'm giving up on Johnny."

"The army has been disbanded. What else can you do? You've been discharged; Johnny will have been discharged as well." Rob didn't say, "If he is still alive," but the words hung between us anyway. After all, it had been nearly two years since he'd gone missing in action. We would have heard by now if he was still alive.

"He's dead, isn't he?"

"Probably," Rob answered.

"I have to know."

"I know. He was my best friend. I want to know, too."

"How will we find out?"

"I don't know. But we'll figure it out."

We walked for six weeks back to Georgia, stopping only to eat and sleep. Sometimes we'd be lucky and find someone willing to share their meager supply of food with us or a farmer who would offer us shelter for the night.

Along the way, we decided the best plan would be for us each to go to our own homes. After we discovered how our families had come through the war, Rob would come to my home and we would decide what to do from there. I was concerned about making a new plan to find Johnny from my home because I knew Father would want to be a part of the plan. Rob told me it was important to include my family in our plans—besides, he wanted to talk to my Father anyway. I felt myself blush when Rob said that; I knew he probably wanted to ask Father for permission to marry me.

Rob's plantation was only fifteen miles from mine, so we walked together most of the way home. It was heartbreaking to go south and see how badly the war had devastated the land. Fields that once were full of crops were burned or overrun by weeds. Buildings seemed neglected, if they hadn't been burned or pulled down.

People were more leery of strangers. Throughout the journey home, we encountered men who had lost limbs in the war. It was discouraging to see these changes.

I was also discouraged about Johnny. Rob said we'd find a way to discover what had happened to him. I couldn't see how we possibly could find him. Every time I passed a man—especially one in uniform—I'd study his face, the way he walked, his voice if he was talking or singing. I was still looking for my brother; maybe I would find him on the road home. Maybe, as had happened in the wilderness, units had gotten intermixed and he'd been fighting all this time with another company. I tried not to listen to the little voice in my head that wondered why he didn't write home.

The more faces I studied, the more convinced I became that Johnny wouldn't look exactly how I remembered him. The soldiers looked older, tired, and wrinkled. I'd study Rob and count the ways he had changed since I'd first met him at Orange County Court House. The crow's feet around his eyes were more pronounced from squinting while marching into the sun. He was thinner and his eyes seemed to be set deeper in his face, more sunken into his head. He was still handsome, but he was different.

I thought of some of the other men I'd fought with and tried to remember how they had looked when I first met them. Mac was much thinner, and Steve Jones had grown a thick beard. In Tom, the difference was more subtle; he didn't sing as much, or smile. Did we all wear the hardships of war where others could see? Maybe Alan, the Yankee soldier I was convinced was a girl, used to smile instead of glare. I was sure she hadn't started smoking a pipe until after she'd joined the army.

Each evening, as I was falling asleep, I tried to imagine how Johnny might look now. Would he still walk with the same energy, as if he was in a hurry to get wherever he was going? Would his hair be longer? Would he have grown a beard? Would his eyes still smile or would they be tired and dull?

Two miles from home, Rob left me to go the extra miles west toward his own house.

"I hate having you walk the rest of the way by yourself. Maybe I'll just go check on my family later and go on home with you now," Rob said.

"I know everyone who lives in this area. What could happen?" I replied.

"I don't even want to think about it."

"I'll be perfectly safe."

"I'm not worried about you getting home from here. I'm worried you'll come up with another crazy plan and run off to endanger your life again," he said teasingly.

"I promise I'll wait for you before I act on another crazy plan."

"You better!"

He gave me a hug and one last kiss. I stood and watched him until he was almost around the bend. He turned and stood motionless for a moment, then slowly raised his hand to salute me. I returned his salute, then turned away. As I took my first step away from Rob, I became excited for him to see me again, but in fancy shoes instead of army boots.

ᘓ

As I walked up the hard-packed dirt of the drive in front of my home, I was surprised at how glad I was to be home. I noticed every drooping shutter and the peeling paint, but never had a house looked so beautiful to me as the evening sun shone on it. The front door was wide open and I could see down the wide hall that the back door also was open, trying to let any breeze come through and cool the house.

I was halfway down the drive when a man stepped onto the porch. I knew it wasn't Father; this man was taller and much thinner than Father. He came down the four wide porch steps and watched me approach. *Who is this? Had Mother and Father sold the place while I was gone?*

I was about five feet away when the man spoke. "You on your way home, kid? We can probably find some food for you, and there is a place to sleep in the barn."

I stopped as soon as he spoke. I knew that voice! His face was so thin that his cheeks looked hollow. Around his gray eyes there were deeply etched lines and the hair at his temples had faded from dark brown to gray. Even with the changes, I recognized him. Without a word, I dropped my bedroll and started running to him ready to throw myself into his arms.

I must have looked crazy because Johnny's eyes widened in alarm as I started toward him. When I was less than a foot away he swept his right leg out in an arch along the ground, catching my left ankle. My next vision was of the clouds as I landed in the dirt on my back. As I caught my breath, Johnny came and stood over me with his hands bunched into fists and a fierce glare on his face.

"Get out of here!"

He doesn't know who I am. All this time I'd been picturing the changes in Johnny's face so I would recognize him when I saw him, and now he didn't recognize me. I started laughing. Not once had I thought Johnny wouldn't know me—even dressed in boy's clothing.

Johnny's eyes went wide. He relaxed his fists and said, "Sammie Annie?"

I swept his legs out from under him as I rolled out of the way, dropping him the same way he'd dropped me. I'd learned more than drills in my two years in a camp full of men.

"Who else would it be?" I asked. I started laughing again, in relief that I'd found my brother alive and home. He laughed with me, rolling up on his elbow looking down at me.

"Where'd you get such a pretty dress?" he asked, indicating my tattered uniform full of fleas and lice.

"They give them to you for free when you join the army. Hadn't you heard?"

Giving a lock of my chopped hair a gentle tug, he said, "I can't honestly say this is the best look for you."

"I got tired of spending so much time putting it up. Besides, hairpins give me a headache." I smiled at him.

Rolling onto his back beside me, he asked as we watched the clouds slide by, "Where have you been, Sammie Annie?"

"In the Georgia 14th. Where have you been?"

"Healing from a bullet that lodged in my hip. I ended up in Pennsylvania at the home of some nice Yankees."

"What!" I exclaimed as I sat up.

"Not all Yankees are bad. Most of them are just like us." I lay back down on the dirt and remembered the times we snuck out of our trenches at night to trade tobacco for food. I thought of Alan and wondered if Johnny knew just how "like me" some of the Yankees had been. "I know. I met some, too."

"Well, those Yankees took me in and cared for me until I was well enough to get around on my own. By then winter had set in and they insisted I stay until the snow had passed so I didn't get sick."

I was glad he'd stayed through the winter, remembering all the snow that had fallen in the Shenandoah Valley. If it was that cold in Tennessee, it would have been much worse farther north in Pennsylvania.

"Their neighbors didn't mind that they were caring for a 'Reb'?" I asked, trying to picture the anger that would have engulfed our area if someone had been helping a Yank. I shuttered at what might have happened—threats, and probably worse.

"Their neighbors didn't know. I mostly stayed out of the way when people came to call, and I absolutely never said anything when I saw someone who wasn't in that Yankee family. Those people have a huge accent."

I understood that. Sometimes, when I heard a Yank talk, I could hardly tell what they were trying to say.

"Then what?" I asked.

"I helped them with the spring planting because their boys were fighting in the war. Then I had to work my way south. I had to be careful because a lot of those Northerners would have been happy to send a southern boy to a prison camp or the grave. It didn't help any that General Grant's army kept moving south."

"Yes, I know. Every time we thought we'd have them stopped, they'd go around us."

"I guess you do know. I bet that was a frustrating time. Some of those men would have been a real pain to deal with when you were losing ground."

"We were all discouraged. I can't say it was much fun, but I preferred the little skirmishes and the marches to fighting in a big battle."

"Amen to that."

"So you got through enemy territory, then what?"

"By the time I caught up to the edge of Yankee-controlled territory, it was winter again. I went across the lines at night, which was the most difficult part of the whole thing. I didn't know if the Yankees would shoot me in the back for being a deserter or our army would shoot me in the front for being a Yankee. It didn't help that I was in civilian clothes, so either side could have thought I was a spy."

I shuttered to think of how terrifying that time must have been for Johnny. If I'd learned anything during the war, it was that everyone got scared. Even brave people like Johnny.

"Then I came on home, only to find my baby sister gone. Why'd you do it, Sammie Annie? Why join up?"

"I went looking for you."

"And now you found me."

"And now I found you."

In silence, we watched the clouds floating above us. Finally Johnny said, "So, little sister, start at the beginning."

ABOUT THE AUTHOR

~

Born in Provo, Utah, Anne and her family moved around the western United States before settling in Missoula, Montana. She is still an ardent fan of the Big Sky country.

Anne left Montana in 1991 to attend Brigham Young University. She graduated in 1995 with a bachelor's degree in business.

Anne and husband Mark have moved 11 times in their first 15 years of marriage, including two and a half years in Duesseldorf, Germany. They can include two stays in Denver and two in Georgia among the places they have lived. While in Georgia, Anne fell in love with all things Civil War related. Anne spent many hours researching and visiting Civil War battlefields and museums. From there, her imagination really took off and Anne began writing historical fiction to tell the stories of how it might have been.

DISCUSSION QUESTIONS

~

1. Samantha Anne left the comfort of everything she knew to go and search for her older brother, Johnny. Why did she leave? Is there anyone you would take a similar risk for? Who? Why would you take that risk?

2. After Samantha Anne joined the army, she rarely talks about her parents again. Why do you think that was?

3. The 14th Georgia Infantry did not go into battle for several months after Samantha Anne joined up. Was this an advantage or disadvantage to Sam? In a similar situation, would you prefer to have your "first battle" behind you quickly or to have more time to become comfortable in your new surroundings?

4. Mac did not respect Sam when she first came to camp. Why do you think he picked on Sam specifically? How did her day as an orderly help her earn Mac's respect?

5. How would you feel if you were Sam and your messmates had played the joke with the chicken dinner? What do you think your reaction would have been?

6. When Sam realized how difficult it was going to be to find Johnny, she thought about confessing to General Thomas. Do you think she should have turned herself in? What do you think General Thomas' reaction would have been? What kind of experiences would she have had if he'd sent her to prison, what experiences might she have had if the General had sent her home?

7. What contributed to Sam's decision to stay in the Confederate Army? What contributed to her longing to go?

8. During Sam's time in the army, her attitude about battle changed, why do you think her that was?

9. Of all the things that Sam faced, what do you think was the worst?

10. Do you think Rob knew Sam was a girl from the time he met her, or did he figure it out later? Why did he wait to tell her he knew? Why did Rob want Sam to confess her gender to him?

11. Why was Samantha Anne angry with Rob when he told her to tell General Thomas she was a girl? Do you think her anger was justified?

12. How do you think Samantha Anne's parents felt when they discovered she was missing? Do you think they tried to find her? What do you think their reactions were when Sam came home? Should Sam have contacted them during her time away?

13. When Johnny got home and found Samantha Anne gone how do you think he felt? Do you think he had any ideas about where she was?

14. At the end of the book, Samantha Anne was returning to the life of a civilian lady. Do you think it would be difficult to return to being the youngest daughter? Would it be as difficult to transform back into a girl as it was to transform into a boy? What "male" privileges would she miss as a woman?

15. Who was your favorite character? Why? Who was your least favorite character? Why? Which characters do you wish knew more about?